DESIRE

Fileata
imaginative fiction

Second edition published March 2019
by Fileata Fiction.

Copyright ©2018 by Seán De Siun. All rights reserved.

Cover: Tooreen, Goleen near Skibbereen, Co Cork,
photograph by Seán De Suin

No part of this publication may be reproduced, stored
in a retrieval system, transmitted in any form or otherwise
circulated, uploaded to the internet or transmitted by email or
any other means, reproduced in any form without the proir
written permission of the publisher.

This book is a work of fiction any resemblance to events or
people past or present is absolutely amazing, but is wholly
a product of the author's imagination.

A CIP record for this book is available
from National LIbrary of Australia

ISBN 978-0-9806049-9-3

COPY SALES

The Curator is available on www.amazon.com
Purchase direct from www.fileata.co

Distribution enquiries:
Fileata Fiction

sales@fileata.co
www.fileata.co

Fileata
imaginative fiction

DESIRE

Set in West Cork, Ireland from 1914 to the struggle for independence in 1920, Desire is a dramatisation of the events that led to the birth of a nation, the Republic of Ireland.

Seen through the eyes of one young man whose life seems destined to carry him to the heart of the struggle, Desire is based on the real story of a member of the Flying Columns, a participant in the guerilla war that led to the British withdrawal from Ireland.

Desire explores the reasons and motivations for the dramatic events of the time, from the onset of World War 1 to the Easter Rising and the battle of Kilmichael that turned the tide of the Irish War of Independence in the direction of the nationalists.

By

Seán De Siun

Author's note

My wish in writing this book is to bring to life the dramatic birth of a nation from the viewpoint of one man and free it from the confines of dry historical statements.

I have attempted to understand the reasons and motivations for the events that took place one hundred years ago and more, and put the reader in the shoes of the people of the time, in particular, my grand-uncle Ned.

This work is neither intended as an historical account, nor have I tried to personify the real man, whom I did not know. It is purely my attempt to walk in his shoes and understand those times and what his experiences, thoughts and desires may have been, and to tell his story.

The accounts of specific events such as Easter 1916 and Kilmichael are based on Ned's statement to the Bureau of Military History in 1956. I have followed what he stated he did and saw.

All the other events are fictional. Some of the main characters are based on historical figures (Ned's parents and family, Tom Barry) but in no way represent the actual people. They are fictional renderings.

I never met my grand-uncle, his parents or brother (my grandfather). I had the pleasure of meeting and communicating with his son Johnny, as well as many members of the extended family including Ned's nephew, my father.

As to the history, I have attempted to condense a great deal of information into a few paragraphs to give the reader an impression of the social and political background of the times. Other people may have a different take on events and I do not claim that my version is comprehensive, complete or correct. However, I have tried to take a balanced view and understand the situation at the time, and put it into context to gain an understanding of how the protagonists' perception of Irish history and the unfolding events of their time influenced their thoughts and actions.

I dedicate this book to my mother and father and the people of West Cork.
SDS

1

The image was bright, alive and real. His mother Margaret was dressed as always in black. She stood with her back to him, her tiny frame hunched over an enormous cauldron. Her two little hands, wrapped around a huge wooden spoon, stirred an iridescent liquid. Flame danced out from underneath the pot. Steam wafted from its boiling contents.

She turned her face to look at him and smiled. Her eyes pierced him as she said, 'Don't worry Ned, you'll be alright. Just remember what I've always told you. Forgive, you must forgive or you'll not be forgiven yourself.'

Ned moved towards the gleaming cauldron and felt the heat radiating from its rounded belly. He stood behind his mother, towering over her. He looked down on her neatly combed and braided brown hair, her shoulders pushing and pulling, rhythmically stirring the pot.

'Do you want to get in, do you? Go on Ned, jump in, you'll be lovely and warm.'

'No, Ma. No, I can't. I'll boil to death in there,' he whispered.

'Not at all,' she scolded, 'Sure, it'll make a new man of ye it will.'

She turned her searching eyes towards him full of love, compassion and tears. 'Two wrongs don't make a right; remember that as well, my son.'

With a jolt, his head shaking, shoulders pushed upwards, he awoke. He opened his eyes but there was no light, just darkness. Soon, a finger of sunlight pushed beneath the bedroom door and danced up the wall and before long he was fully awake in the early morning gloom.

He had experienced this dream before. It roused a distant memory, the feeling, smell and presence of his mother. It was as if he could hear her breathing, almost singing, humming to him when he was a baby in his cot.

'Peaceful you are now, my darling boy. No worries have ye and none you ever will have, please God. Hush now to sleep my angel, child of ours, gift of God, eternal, full of grace and ever you shall remain. God loves you and so do all of us here on God's earth. You are in the arms of Mother Ireland, so have no fears, my child. At the end of time we will all be one, together with Christ in heaven, united, pure. Hush, little child. Go to sleep, little baby, sleep.'

His mother had passed as all things must, forty years ago. He had missed her soft voice and gentle ways for what seemed an eternity. Now, as an old man himself, he imagined she was closer to him than she had been across the ocean of time, between then and now. Time collapsed; there were so many memories. What difference did the order, the exact moment that they had taken place, make? They were nothing but memories now, distant, down the corridor of time.

Slowly, he pushed himself out of bed and got ready for the day. A few hours later he sat in the church with his son Johnny and his wife Kathleen. Good turnout, he thought, everyone is here. One by one, figures from the past gave eulogies from the lectern.

All agreed – Tom Barry was an Irish hero. He was a hero indeed, that's true, thought Ned.

Tired, he closed his eyes and his thoughts drifted back to his dream, his mother, 'Grandma of the Green' as his extended family and the townspeople of Dunmanway called her in the old days. 'She'll have a golden staircase to heaven,' they used to say.

'Ned, come to me now,' she called through the open door of the shop. He threw down his fag end, crossed West Green and went inside to see what she needed him for.

His eyes adjusted to the darkness. Standing in the doorway, he turned his head to the right and looked into the shop where his mother stood behind the counter. She was carefully weighing thick, moist, brown sugar and putting it into dark grey bags. There was a large tea chest on her side of the counter and she added a filled bag to a neat row she had made on top of it. He looked left into the harness making workshop to see the silhouette of his father Thomas, crouched over and sitting on his stool.

'Your father wants ye,' she said barely raising her eyes to see him.

Thomas was waxing a thick thread attached to an awl. He pushed the awl into a leather strap to make a hole then pulled it through, reaching his arm up high until the thread was taught.

'Will you go down to the fair field and check to see if the beer tent has been set up yet?' he asked. 'The McSweenys said they would put it up this morning.'

'Right you are,' said Ned and made his way down West Green to the fair field. As he approached he heard the buzz of activity, as this was the week before Ballabuidhe, pronounced balla-bwee.

Lúnasa, the Gaelic festival marking the beginning of the harvest season, had been held all over Ireland in pre-Christian times. When Christianity came, the name lost its meaning, and by the Middle Ages a patchwork of festivals across the island with different themes had taken its place. The Famine of the 1840s saw a big decline and many local fairs were lost, however, Ballabuidhe, held in Dunmanway at the beginning of August, kept going strong. A major component of the fair was a horse market. It was no doubt the horse-trading that kept Ballabuidhe alive even during the hardest times

For a few days before the fair proper got underway, dealers brought their stock to the fair field and horse-trading took place. The British army in particular valued the fair. This year, after a quiet few years their agents were there in force buying hundreds of animals. Horses were sold in large lots and lines of them streamed out of the fair field to the station yards and onto railway carriages. As sellers arrived more horses clip-clopped through the streets to the fair.

On his way Ned stopped and bought a Cork Examiner from the paperboy. Throughout July the newspapers were full of reports of the impending European war. It was 30 July 1914. Ominously, the headline read –

Austria Declares War against Serbia

We have enough problems of our own, he thought. It all seemed so distant, removed from the immediate problems that Ireland faced.

The British parliament, including the Irish Parliamentary Party, known as the Home Rule Party, was locked in debate over the Government of Ireland Act 1914, known as Home Rule. If the act ever became law, Ireland would be given its own parliament in Dublin and control of most government functions, but remain part of the overarching United Kingdom. However, the act had been knocked back by the House of Lords twice. Since the Reform Act of 1911, once a bill was passed by the

House of Commons for a third time, it did not need the approval of the Lords to be passed into law. In May the House of Commons had for a third time voted in favour of the act, so in theory, it should now receive the Royal Assent and become law.

However, the act had so far not been made into law. So Ireland appeared to be as far as ever from home rule, let alone independence. Ned put the paper in his back pocket and continued to the fair field.

Ballabuidhe was to open two days later and the build-up was taking place. Thousands of people from all over Cork would be coming and Thomas, as he did each year, had a concession for a beer tent. Ned found their site nestled in among several other drinks and food concessions. The McSweeney boys had put the tent up alright, so now the work of stocking it could begin. Dray loads of ale and porter were hauled in large wooden casks direct from the breweries. Thomas' tent always sold Beamish Stout, brewed in Cork City.

A Beamish dray pulled up on the far side of the field, so he made his way over to talk to the driver. He kept his distance as he skirted the four large snorting horses, kicking their hoofs in the grass and sweating after their journey. He had a quick word with the driver and made sure he knew where to make his delivery.

On the outskirts of the field and on the road sides outside town, Travellers had set up camps with their elaborately decorated wagons. They traded horses and also provided metalworking services. During Ballabuidhe the women of Dunmanway and district would have all of their kitchenware repaired, sharpened and cleaned. So from August to Christmas you were in danger of injuring yourself while cutting a slice of bread.

Every spare room in town and in the surrounding localities, especially Nedineagh to the east where the original, ancient Ballabuidhe grounds were located, was filling up with visitors. Relatives, friends, sellers and buyers came from as far afield as Belfast, Liverpool and London. In recent years, natives of the area who had emigrated to America were also reappearing on 'pilgrimages back to Mother Ireland'. August was the busiest month of the year, with non-stop parties and family occasions, especially during Ballabuidhe week, of course.

Ned walked back up into town and ran into his brother Jack on Quarry Road. 'Let's have a pint, Ned,' said Jack.

Ned was the youngest of seven children – at least, he was the youngest now, since his baby sister had died as a child. He was the only one still living with his parents. Jack was four years older than him and had been studying to be a teacher up in Dublin. He had graduated in June and was now back in Dunmanway.

They sat alone in a corner of the Doheny Bar on West Green, a few doors away from the shop. Jack was excited, but in the usual style of West Cork he did his best to cover it up and act normally. Speaking quietly out of the corner of his mouth he said, 'We're starting a Dunmanway unit of the Irish Volunteers. Don't worry, I've already put your name down. We want to recruit as many members as we can during Ballabuidhe.'

'Right, Jack. What do you want me to do?'

'Volunteers are here from Cork with enlistment forms. We just have to talk to all the boys when they're in town and sign them up. We'll have our first meeting at the end of the week,' he said and took a sip of his pint. He could hardly control the smile from pulling across his face.

'It's a serious enough business, Jack.'

'Of course it is, but I'm just relieved that we're finally doing something. After all, the aim of the Volunteers is "to secure the rights and liberties common to all the people of Ireland". We need to get organised here in Dunmanway. I feel as though we've wasted six months already.'

Jack had been talking about joining the Volunteers for nearly a year and assumed that Ned would join as well. After all, he always followed his elder brother's lead. But Ned had no real interest in joining. He was too busy with his work and trying to find his way in the world, not to mention a wife.

He felt a stirring of desire in his innermost self for something different. The image of a boat, a currach with him on the oars pulling along the ocean waves, flickered before his eyes, almost tangible. There was a beautiful girl, her long hair swirling around her shoulders in the breeze, her arms clasping a shawl to her breast. She smiled at him, looking him straight in the eye, mischievous, desirous. She loved him.

Ned was brought back from his daydream with a thud. Jack had finished his drink and with a bold gesture slammed his glass on the table, slapped his knee with his hat and stood up quickly, as if to meet a foe.

'Come on, Ned, we've plenty to do. No time for shilly shallying.'

He was always a man for the bold gesture, thought Ned. He purposefully finished his drink, followed Jack up the street.

Jack was always well dressed in a tidy suit and tie with his jacket button done up. He strode down the street with a confident air, his thick brown hair bouncing with each step.

Ned was rougher than his brother, with strong arms and large hands. He was no taller than Jack, but slim. They both had strong, fast legs from playing Gaelic football and hurling, but Ned had a more relaxed, country gait and nonchalant way about him. With a full lower lip and lively, wide eyes and steady gaze, he seemed self contained, whereas Jack was more outwardly focused and impulsive, as if he was going to burst forth at any time.

On Saturday morning, Thomas and Ned made their way down to the fair field before dawn. They opened up the tent and waited for the first customers. Travellers' caravans ringed the edges of the field where they and other horse sellers were lining up their stock head to tail, feeding and grooming them. The other concession holders were all waiting and ready as the first rays of sun poked above the horizon.

Soon a steady stream of visitors poured in. Horse agents were the first to arrive, and they wasted no time and immediately started the job of assessing the horses and talking to the sellers. Within a few minutes numerous negotiations were in process. You could stand right next to the seller and buyer and listen intently to what they were saying and not catch a word of it, unless you were from West Cork, that is.

But even Ned and his father had difficulty keeping up with the fast and slurred enunciation of the horse traders. The Travellers spoke their own language, Gammon, as well as some Irish and English in varying local accents, and also spoke their own horse trade jargon. To an outsider it sounded like the Tower of Babel.

When a bargain was made they spat on their hands and made elaborate handshakes, slapping and punching their fists together. Wads of cash emerged and folded notes changed hands surreptitiously. Horses were led away and new ones brought to the front from behind caravans.

The British Army needed agents to facilitate their purchases and would not have been very successful without local help. They didn't have the patience for such negotiations in any case. They just wanted to buy horses and move them out.

This attitude ran parallel with the reasons why, over the centuries, English landlords had become known as absentee landlords. In the aftermath of the Cromwellian war, through the latter half of the 1600s, the land was seized from its owners, divided up and given to a variety of British soldiers and their supporters.

By 1700 Richard Cox had started a linen industry in what grew into the town of Dunmanway. He was one of the framers of the hated Penal Laws that successfully eliminated the remnants of the old Irish landowning class entirely.

The Penal Laws continuously changed over the centuries and were sometimes revoked, then reimposed, enforced or ignored, but always they hung like a sword over the people's heads. In the late 1700s, Irish statesman Edmund Burke wrote that the penal laws were –

> '... a machine of wise and elaborate contrivance, as well fitted for the oppression, impoverishment and degradation of a people, and the debasement in them of human nature itself, as ever proceeded from the perverted ingenuity of man.'

During the centuries that followed, the land was sold and traded to different landlords. The town grew up, roads were built and the railway came to Dunmanway towards the end of the 19th century. But the indigenous locals were largely excluded from these developments, left on the margins.

They were variously prohibited from owning land or animals or engaging in local administration or politics. Their Catholic religion was at times completely banned, forcing them to live secret, hidden lives.

Until the 1903 Land Purchase Act, few Irish farmers owned the land they had worked and lived on through the centuries, but were tenants, and paid rent.

Landlords came and went. Some stayed and mingled with the local people. Others came with families and made new, tight-knit communities of their own. So over time, many English descendants settled in Dunmanway and particularly in the town of Bandon, 18 miles away.

The Land Purchase Act provided government money for tenants to buy their land from the landlords. Within just a few years, hundreds of thousands of acres had been purchased by farmers all over Ireland. By now, many of the locals attending Ballabuidhe were small landholders or at least relatives of landholders, and not tenants. This was a transformation from just ten years earlier.

By mid-morning the fair field was crowded with people, horses, dogs and children. The beer tent was full and Thomas and Ned pulled pints as fast as they could. Other stalls sold apples, oranges, sweets and buns for the children, pigs' trotters called crubeens and carrageen seaweed snacks.

In the late afternoon, horse carts arrived. Often the owners would race each other through the town but, once at the field, they took part in organised races. Bolting around the outskirts of the fair field, two or four gigs raced at a time. Flat horse races followed, then harness races. Finally, as the summer evening drew in, youngsters on Shetland ponies raced as well. In town the pubs were full and the streets crowded with people talking, drinking and smoking.

After closing the beer tent for the night, Ned walked home up West Green. From the street he saw candlelight flickering in the upstairs window of his family home and shadows dancing on the walls through the lace curtains. Matchmaking was taking place. Ned's mother had set aside the upstairs sitting room for matchmaking during the fair as she did each year. The matchmakers, nearly all men, used the room for negotiating marriages. The would-be bride and groom would rarely attend but their relatives, the father, mother or an aunt, would negotiate for them.

On the afternoon of the final day was the Céilí Mór or Grand Dance. Dozens of musicians, playing fiddles, bagpipes and tin whistles filled the centre of the fair field.

One piper that everybody crowded around to hear was Concubhar O'Buacalla, known as the prince of all pipers. People said he played the 'Ceol Sidhe', fairy music.

Ballabuidhe unfolded this way each year, always the same though always a bit different. When the fair was over, an eerie feeling came over the town. The streets were empty of people and horses, but full of discarded paper, cigarette butts and horse droppings. Soon the work of clearing up concluded and Dunmanway settled back into the rhythm of the year.

However, this year was different. The looming war and the ongoing home rule crisis were pushing their way into Ned's life.

2

On the Monday evening of Ballabuidhe as Ned was on his way out of the house, his mother confronted him. With her hands on her hips, her face was stern and determined.

'Ned, you'll not go to that meeting. I forbid it!' she barked at him as well as she could with her bell-like voice.

'Ma, we're all going to the meeting and we are all going to join the Volunteers and that's it.'

'You know your father and I are against this. You mustn't go.'

'The Land League is over, All for Ireland is over. We're joining the Volunteers to defend all Irish people.'

Ned walked briskly out the door and headed to Market Square to meet his brother. 'Jack,' he shouted across the square and walked across to where he was standing.

'Hurry up, Ned, I've already signed up,' said Jack.

As Ned walked into the Shamrock Pub, he saw the door of the back room was closed shut with two men standing to attention in front of it. Jack tapped Ned on the shoulder. 'Off you go,' he said.

The door was opened and he was ushered into the room. Two men were sitting at a table with a large ledger. One looked up at him and said, 'Name?' Moments later, Ned was an Irish Volunteer.

In early 1912, Unionists centred in the counties around the city of Belfast had formed armed militias determined to resist the implementation Home Rule, if it ever came into being. By April that year the Ulster Volunteer Force (UVF) had over 100,000 members.

In November 1913, Irish nationalists responded by setting up the Irish Volunteers 'to secure the rights and liberties common to all the people of Ireland'. The Volunteers included members of the Gaelic League, Ancient Order of Hibernians, the political party Sinn Féin and secretly, the Irish Republican Brotherhood (IRB).

In March 1914 British Army officers at the Army Headquarters in the Curragh Camp, alarmed at the prospect that Home Rule would finally become law, staged a mutiny that became known as the Curragh Incident. With UVF violence and chaos a looming possibility, the British government contemplated military action against them. Senior British officers at the Curragh threatened to resign and said they would refuse to carry out orders to act against the UVF. The head of the army gave them assurances that the army would not be used against Unionists.

This created a terrible fear throughout the rest of Ireland. It became clear that the British Army would not defend the majority of the population, but may well be used against them in support of attacks by the UVF. As a result, thousands of men and boys flocked to join the Irish Volunteers.

Across Ireland, over 150,000 men had signed up by the summer of 1914. In addition, many thousands of women volunteered for the female branch, Cumann na mBan, The Women's Council, including Ned's sister Kit. It seemed that a wave of nationalism had gripped the country.

During July 1914, Europe erupted into turmoil as war was declared by Austria-Hungary and Germany. When the German Army invaded Belgium on 4 August, the British Empire declared war on Germany. Ireland was part of the British Empire and was expected to take part.

In September the Irish Parliamentary Party Leader, John Redmond, who had spent years working for home rule in the British parliament, made a speech to a parade of Irish Volunteers in Wicklow. He urged the Volunteers to join the British Army. He called for the Irish Volunteers to be renamed the National Volunteers and put its efforts into supporting the war.

Just two days earlier the British Parliament had finally passed the Home Rule Act, but they had also immediately suspended it until six months after the war was over, whenever that might be.

Jack scratched his head and said, 'So the idea is that we're to give up our struggle against the English, throw in our lot with them and get killed in a foreign war defending their cursed empire. If any of us are still alive at the end they might make good on their promise and give us a few home rule powers. They must think we're as stupid as they are. Let them fight their own war.'

Ned and Jack were sure that all Volunteers would ignore Redmond. Even Thomas thought Redmond had gone too far. 'Boys, I think he's been sold. Now he's trying to save his ass by selling us. No one in Cork will have a bar of it I can tell you that.'

But he was wrong. At the next Volunteers parade in Dunmanway only three quarters of the company showed up. A sense of excitement filled the parade hall with many of the men talking excitedly about joining the army. Some had already left for Bandon or Cork to enlist.

The Volunteers had a steering committee and Jack was the chairman. He called the men to attention and asked them all to sit down. He said, 'Now we've all heard about Mr Redmond's speech. But this unit was formed to defend the people of Ireland and I am sure that all of you here will not be enlisting, and will stay the course with us here in Ireland.'

There was silence in the room. Men played with their hats and pulled on their cigarettes until one man coughed and said, 'I don't know Jack. I'm going to enlist anyway. We'll be fighting for Ireland alright, and we'll be getting paid for it too – wages that my family needs. I've no land or money. I just can't resist it. We'll have our freedom after the war. It'll all be over by Christmas anyway.'

Murmurs of agreement echoed around the room. Ned shook his head in disbelief. His father had been watching the proceedings from the entrance. He walked up to the front of the room and whispered in Jack's ear. Jack said, 'My father Thomas would like to address you all.'

Thomas pulled himself up to his full height. He was a sturdy straight-backed man with neatly trimmed hair. He wore a short walrus moustache that was now grey. Like his sons, he had gentle, slightly drooping eyes that made him look as if he was listening sympathetically.

He began to speak. 'You all know that for many years I have been a supporter of O'Brien and the Land League. After innumerable years of struggle, O'Brien and the League wrenched reform out of the English. We achieved more for Ireland in the last ten years than O'Connell, Parnell and all the others going back hundreds of years.

'You also know that the policy of O'Brien is not one of confrontation or violence. I do not support physical force because it has never succeeded in defeating the English. O'Brien has achieved more through negotiation than a dozen uprisings. But one thing is for sure. The English have never, and will never, do anything for Ireland unless they are made to.

'What will make them move, and give freedom to Ireland? Not physical force. No, they know too much about that. They equate physical force with power, but have no moral basis for their tyranny and no power over us. For nearly eight hundred years they have tried with all their might to subjugate the Irish people but have failed.

'They have failed precisely because their only weapon has been physical force. But we have the power of right on our side and so have never been defeated. They have always been in the wrong and are therefore doomed to ultimate failure.

'Let us not follow them into this terrible European war, a war to save their evil empire, an empire that will surely pass into the dung heap of history.

'You men should stay in Ireland and see that they make good on their promise of home rule. Otherwise, they will renege on that promise, of that you can be sure. Do you think they will remember us once your job is done and they celebrate their victory? Don't be fooled again.'

Thomas' shoulders slumped and he sighed. He had used all his strength to make his speech. But he was no longer a young man and had given his all to get his words out. He slowly lowered himself down into a chair.

For a moment the room fell silent. But soon the sound of scraping feet and chairs moving grew loud. Mumbles rose in volume like crickets on a summer night. Eventually Jack stood up, tapped the table with his knuckles and said, 'Alright men, enough has been said. Let us continue on with the business of the Volunteers.'

One of the men stood up and said, 'Redmond told us to rename the Volunteers the National Volunteers and support the war effort. That's what we're going to do, those of us who don't join up immediately in any case.'

One by one nearly all the men stood up and walked out. The committee members sat at their table. Ned, Thomas and a dozen or so men remained in their chairs dotted around the room.

One of the seated men, Michael McCarthy, lived in the next street from Ned and his family on East Green. He was a tall dark fellow, a few years younger than Ned. Like Ned and Jack he was in the Gaelic League and the Gaelic Athletic Association (GAA).

He said, 'I can't explain it to myself even. It's just that I have a feeling of excitement deep with in me, a glow, like an ember keeping me warm. But by God it frightens me. I think those boys are going to miss the big show. They think they'll be in the thick of the action fighting with the English.

'For me, anyway, leaving Ireland now would be like leaving the dinner table just before the main course is served. We're close, as close as we've ever been. The ghosts of the past are not gone, they're only sleeping and I feel them stirring me in, telling me to stay the course. But now is the time the rest of the boys choose to abandon us, now of all times.' He shook his head and scrunched his cap in his hand.

Jack always had something to say and always proposed action. Ever since he was a boy, towering over Ned when he was a toddler, Jack would stride forth, 'Come on, Ned boy, let's go to the river, always keep moving, thinking on your feet. No time for shilly shallying.'

Now Jack slammed his fist on the table and declared, 'Well, that's it then, we will just have to start our own new branch of the Irish Volunteers.'

Their numbers reduced from 120 to just 20, but the Irish Volunteers continued to meet. The newly formed National Volunteers held parades as well. But over the course of the winter of 1914-15 their numbers dwindled and by the spring they ceased to exist.

The remaining Irish Volunteers were the subjects of suspicion and hostility in the town. Jack said, 'Never mind, Ned, we'll just keep our necks in, play football and see how things unfold.'

On Saturday mornings, Ned and Jack walked down Quarry Road to the De La Salle School where the GAA met for a football match. On a Saturday in late November they kicked a stone down the road as they walked hands in pockets to the football ground. They paused to read a poster with a picture of John Redmond and the words –

Your first duty is to play your part in ending the war.
Join an Irish Regiment today.

The first groups of men to join the British army were cheered by crowds who sang 'It's a Long Way to Tipperary' as they boarded trains in Cork and Limerick on their way to the war.

Even before Redmond's speech urged men to enlist, Irish soldiers in the British Army were dying. Over three hundred Irish soldiers were killed in the very first battle of the war at Mons in late August 1914.

Hundreds more died at Le Pilly in October and now a battle was raging at Ypres. So far, the casualties were all soldiers who had already been in the army or reserves at the beginning of the war. The new recruits were yet to see action.

As well as death notices, money from the army was flowing and many town folk still supported the war effort and walked with determined faces, glancing away from Ned as they passed him.

He stared at the poster and his stomach clenched. It seemed that the majority of the Irish people, even in his home town of Dunmanway, had sided with and considered themselves part of the British Empire, not Ireland. His sense of national identity and belonging was crushed. He now felt like an outsider, a foreigner in his own home.

In late January, Jack married Margaret McSweeney, who was born at her family farm located just outside of Dunmanway on the original Ballabuidhe site. But soon the wedding was overshadowed by the war.

By the turn of 1915 the papers carried daily lists of the dead. In addition to the established, mostly pro-war press, numerous new newspapers and pamphlets were circulating around town. They were full of invective against Ireland's involvement in the 'English' or 'Imperial War'.

Lorry drivers and railway staff arrived in Dunmanway with the latest editions of what were dubbed the 'mosquito press'. These papers had titles such as *The Irish Volunteer, Nationality, The Worker's Republic* and *The Socialist*, which was founded by James Connolly.

By the spring of 1915 the stream of pro-war propaganda was being undermined by letters from soldiers and medical staff from the front that reached the newspapers. A sense of betrayal grew. The papers used the term 'cannon fodder' and described the 'uncaring incompetence of British generals'.

Canada and Australia had also joined the war and many of their casualties were of Irish descent. In West Cork it seemed as if the war was being fought and lost on the bloodied backs of the Irish.

When the disaster of the Gallipoli campaign unfolded, Ireland went into collective shock. On 25 April 1915 the 1st battalion of the Royal Munster Fusiliers and the 1st battalion of the Royal Dublin Fusiliers were slaughtered when they tried to come ashore at V Beach during the first day of the Gallipoli landings.

Hundreds of men were killed, trapped in the SS River Clyde as it attempted to land them. On the other side of V Beach, three companies of the Royal Dublin Fusiliers attempted to come ashore in rowing boats towed in by barges. The boats drifted broadside onto the Turkish machine guns and the men were slaughtered, with 600 killed or maimed.

At the same time at Ypres the 2nd Royal Dublin Fusiliers suffered 500 casualties. In May at Mouse Trap Farm, the Germans fired shells loaded with chlorine gas at the Irish lines. Only 21 of the 658 men survived.

Ned and Jack sat in the Doheny Bar and read the Cork Echo editorial –

... Every one of us knows an Irish mother or wife bereaved or has a brother or son who will never return ...

Nevertheless, the mainstream press continued in its patriotic support of the 'Empire in its fight for the small nations of the world'.

'So we're not a small nation worth fighting for?' said Ned.

Jack took a sip of whiskey, looked out into West Green from the window of the Doheny Bar and said, 'We'll bide our time, Ned. There are moves on the way. England's calamity is our opportunity.'

'Jack, this is Ireland's calamity we're witnessing.'

'It is indeed, one more terrible waste of Irish blood. But they all volunteered. Foolish as they were, I feel ashamed that we weren't there to aid them in some way,' said Jack pulling on his cigarette.

In June, Jeremiah O'Donovan Rossa, the feared and despised – by the English – Fenian, died in New York at the age of 83. Ned read his biography for the first time in the newspaper.

He was born in Rosscarbery not twenty miles from Dunmanway, fifteen years before the Great Famine of 1845-49. He descended from an ancient Irish family that had been dispossessed during the Cromwellian invasion of Ireland. He had survived three wives, all from West Cork, and fathered eighteen children.

In 1865, he was arrested for plotting the Fenian uprising and sentenced to life in prison. While imprisoned in England, he was elected in absentia to the British Parliament as member for Tipperary. The next year he and several other plotters were pardoned but exiled and went to the United States.

In New York he joined the Fenian Brotherhood who traced their origins to the uprising of 1798 and Wolfe Tone. There he published The United Irishman newspaper, which extolled the use of physical force and armed rebellion to gain Irish independence.

Eventually the Fenian Brotherhood had merged with the Irish Republican Brotherhood (IRB), a secret society dedicated to the establishment of an independent, democratic, Irish republic – through the use of physical force. Jack always winked at Ned when their name was mentioned, and he knew that they were the real organisers behind the Irish Volunteers.

The IRB arranged for O'Donovan Rossa's body to be returned to Ireland and staged a hero's funeral for him. On 1 August, the first day of Ballabuidhe, a huge tumult of people turned out to witness his funeral procession.

Thousands of Irish Volunteers lined the streets of Dublin as the hearse carrying his coffin passed through the city from the Pro-Cathedral to Glasnevin Cemetery. Hundreds of thousands of Dubliners lined the route. After Rossa was laid in his grave, the famous poet, writer, nationalist, prominent political activist and IRB member, Pádraig Pearse gave a graveside oration that was carried in the newspapers the following day –

> ... Our foes are strong and wise and wary... They think that they have pacified Ireland. They think that they have purchased half of us and intimidated the other half. They think that they have foreseen everything, think that they have provided against everything; but, the fools, the fools, the fools! They have left us our Fenian dead, and while Ireland holds these graves, Ireland unfree shall never be at peace ...

'Gasbag,' said Ned.

'Not at all,' said Jack, 'Sure he's a great poet and orator and those prophetic words will give tremendous gravitas to our cause.'

Ned had only a vague idea of who O'Donovan Rossa was until his death. His was a name you heard now and then when people talked about the old days. Now, having read his biography, Ned understood that he had 'skin in the fight'. It was clear that neither O'Donovan Rossa nor his extended family, many of whom were to be easily found living across West Cork, had ever forgotten the past cruelty and oppression meted out to them.

His ancestral family had been destroyed. They died by the

roadside of starvation, forced to eat heather. The shattered remnants of his family had endured the Penal Laws. The survivors had rallied and suffered the landlordism of the nineteenth century and witnessed the famines of 1845-49 when large areas of Ireland were depopulated by starvation, forced evictions and mass migration.

The biography fascinated him. He didn't mind reading, but he had never read a book except at school. Jack was different. He was always reading poetry, Shakespeare or something.

Ned had never read any history books or historical literature, although he knew all the local oral history. Helping his mother in the shop while her customers chatted, or sitting in the harness making workshop, he heard local farmers speaking under their breath about who owed what to whom and how and where and why. He had heard all the local trials and tribulations a hundred times.

But it seemed a new world was opened up to him by reading the mosquito press newspapers and pamphlets that were everywhere now. He read a slew of papers of varying political persuasions, interspersed with historical references, and after a while he was able to piece together the history of Ireland since Cromwellian times.

It was only while O'Donovan Rossa was exiled in America that the beginnings of democracy and land reform finally began to ease the burden of the mass of the Irish people. It was clear to Ned that reform did not come due to the largesse or decency of the ruling class. It came through the determined and energetic striving of individuals including Daniel O'Connell, Charles Parnell, William O'Brien and the now discredited, democratically elected leader of the Home Rule Party, John Redmond.

Ned read an editorial in The Fenian –

> ... *Obstinate, recalcitrant, immovable, since the 1880s in the face of the clear and democratic expression of the Irish people, the English populace, through their elected and hereditary parliament, have denied Ireland its democratically expressed will for independence ...*

In May, Ned read a warning from Pearce —

> ...What if conscription be enforced on Ireland? What if a Unionist or a Coalition British Ministry repudiates the Home Rule Act? What if it be determined to dismember Ireland? The future is big with these and other possibilities...

No, home rule was not enough. It had never been enough. The promise of the English was worthless unless enforced, and who was going to make them keep their word? Ned wanted more, like his brother Jack and like all the others in the Irish Volunteers, he wanted more, and the funeral of O'Donnovan Rossa had clarified his thinking.

.

3

In July, as Dunmanway prepared for the next Ballabuidhe, horses were being brought in from all over the southwest of Ireland. The army desperately needed as many horses as it could acquire. Indeed, the whole farming environment had picked up due to the war and the insatiable demand for produce, milk and meat it created. As a result farm gate prices had increased and business in town was brisk. People seemed relieved to think about something other than the war. But the merriment came to a shuddering stop when, in mid-August, news filtered through from Gallipoli.

In August the 10th Irish Division, made up of new volunteers who had enlisted since Redmond's speech, were slaughtered at Sulva Bay. The soldiers in the division had come from all strata of Irish life. Many were middle class city people and the news of their deaths reverberated across Ireland.

Until Sulva Bay, terrible as it was, the war had remained outside normal experience. Now the seriousness of the tragedy struck home to everyone. Thomas was deeply affected by it. Ned sat in his usual spot on his stool in the corner of the workshop. Three local farmers sat around with Thomas on his chair, hands on his knees, as Ned read the newspaper aloud to them.

'Sure by God, Ned, I missed the death of the famine years, and I hoped I would never bear witness to such loss,' said Thomas.

His father was shocked by the description of the carnage. But Ned felt a strange calm. 'I'm glad I missed that one,' he said to his mother.

'Make sure you miss them all,' she replied.

Ned remembered one near miss when he a boy. He was fourteen years old. School had closed for the summer. Thomas summoned Jack and Ned and said, 'During the holidays you two boys will go down to Nedinagh and help your grandma O'Brien on the farm, all right?'

Jack said, 'Yerra, it means we're to have no fun this summer, Ned. It means we have to work mucking pigs and diggin' spuds.'

The Nedinagh farmlands are to the east of town where their mother was born. Grandma O'Brien, her eldest son and his wife and children lived on a farm that had been in the family for generations. Going back into the distant past, the O'Briens had been tenant farmers in Nedinagh. When the Land Act gave them the opportunity to purchase their land they didn't hesitate.

The Land Act was the result of years of agitation by William O'Brien, a Member of Parliament and founder of the All-for-Ireland League. He was from Mallow, thirty miles from Dunmanway. O'Brien had spent decades pursuing land reform that culminated in the 1903 Land Act. The act's purpose was to enable tenant farmers to purchase their land. The government paid the difference in the prices asked for by the landlord and the amount the farmer was able to pay.

The Land Act was enormously successful, especially in County Cork, and thousands of farmers changed from tenants to land owners. The O'Brien's of Nedinagh were among the first to in the West Cork to complete their purchase.

Jack and Ned had walked to the farm many times before, and they took their usual route. When they came to the train station Ned stepped on the left rail of the track and walked along the top of it one foot directly in front of the other with his arms outstretched. Jack did likewise on the right rail, but after a few steps he jumped off the rail and walked in the middle of the track. The railway line was a shorter way to get to Nedinagh than taking the road.

Ned kept walking along on the rail. The aim was to see if he could get all the way across the Bandon River without falling off. The two of them had done this many times, but Jack was now too grown up for such antics.

Jack stooped down to grab a handful of stones that lined the track. They walked, Ned toeing along the rail, Jack taking long steps to keep on the sleepers. Jack threw one stone as far down the track as he could, attempting to hit the top of the rail and see the stone fly off at an angle. Ping, one stone hit its target and flew off at a tangent. 'Got it', shouted

Jack and threw another while in full stride, ping, 'and another!'

Jack was always competitive. Nothing could happen in his sphere that didn't involve some sort of test of strength or skill.

They had nearly reached the river and Ned had managed to keep on the rail. Jack was just ahead of him and stopped to see if he could hit a bird with a stone. 'Aragh, missed it', he exclaimed.

'What do you want to hit a bird for anyway, Jack?'

'That was a fat wood pigeon and it would have made nice eating.'

Jack threw another stone up the tracks and it pinged off the rail, followed by a loud howl.

'Ouch! Who threw that stone? Wait till I get ye!'

They stopped and Ned fell off the rail. They peered up the tracks and saw three boys walking towards them in a line. Jack said, 'I recognise them. They're from Ballynacarriga.'

The three boys grimaced, picked up stones and hurled them down the track. Ned turned to run, but Jack called, 'Ned, hold your ground, don't show them any fear. We have to stand up to them. This is our town.'

Ned cowered behind Jack who stared in their direction. One stone hit Jack on the leg, another on his chest. He flinched in pain but didn't move.

The boys started running toward them. 'We'll kill ye,' shouted one of them his face contorted in anger.

'We're outnumbered Jack, let's go,' said Ned his voice shaking in fear.

'We're not outnumbered now,' said a calm voice behind him. Jack and Ned turned around to see Michael McCarthy.

Michael was younger than but just as tall as Ned. His shirt sleeves were rolled up above his outsized biceps, and he clenched his fists and shook his right hand at the attackers who were now just a few yards away. He pushed Jack out of the way and stepped towards the first boy.

The three boys, all older than Michael, slowed down and raised their fists. The first one swung at Michael who ducked the blow, and swung back hitting the boy in the chin. He fell straight down, his head cracking on the rail, knocked out.

The other two boys dropped to their knees. 'Christ, you've bloody well killed me brother.' They frantically patted the downed boy on the cheeks and blew in his face. After a few seconds he revived and said, 'Whaaa happened?'

Softly, Michael said, 'You messed with lads from Dunmanway, that's what happened.'

From that day on, Ned kept out of fights. He never forgot the fear he felt as his enemies approached, determined to harm him. He was still ashamed that he had not thought of defending his brother but only keeping out of the way of the stones, even if it meant using his brother as a shield. After that day, he told himself, never get into a fight. Keep away from all trouble.

Since then, nine years before, he had held Michael McCarthy in awe. He realised that day that his brother was brave, but Michael was a warrior.

The three farmers left and Thomas picked up his needle and resumed his work sewing a horse collar. Carefully, slowly, in perfect rhythm he pushed the big needle through the leather and pulled it out the other side.

When Ned had left school, he became his father's apprentice in the saddlery. That was seven years ago and now, like his father, he was a fully qualified harness maker. Ned picked up *The Harness Makers' Guide* and turned to the page for a Cart Horse Headstall to look up the standard measurements for the brace and throat pieces. He had an order for two headstalls that had to be completed the next week.

It seemed ironic to him that his father, who had no land, should be so proud of his association with the Land League and its achievements. Thomas' family was from Drinagh, a few miles from Dunmanway. He was born in 1859 in the long shadow of the famine. As he was the youngest son, the farm on which they were tenants had gone to his older brother, and he became a harness maker.

'Promise me you'll keep out of the fight to come, will you?' Thomas said across his shoulder, casting a half glance at Ned.

'Well, I kept out of the war, Da, so far anyway.'

'You'd never enlist, to be sure.'

'Of course not, but who knows, they might try to conscript us. They're going to run out of men to send to their deaths soon enough.'

'You know the fight I'm talking about – our fight. I was for the Volunteers at first, the idea of defending us against outside attack. Under those circumstances, what else can you do? But now there are murmurs of us taking action. To what end? Don't we have our Land Act, the Housing Act? One day, the next step will be taken, home rule.'

'Da, I don't want to fight. But as you said yourself, the English will never keep their word unless we force them. After this war is over, who knows if any of the leaders who voted for home rule will be left? As Pearse said, "The future is big with these and other possibilities."'

'Ned, I still believe that, as O'Brien said, only through parliamentary reform, constitutionally, with power of the press and public opinion behind us, can we bring positive change. We can't act outside society, and we cannot afford any more victims.'

Ned thought, he's trotting out the same old lines I've been hearing since I was a baby. I agree with him though. We don't need any more victims.

Thomas continued, 'My involvement with the Land League broadened my horizons. I learned about politics – I mean, relating to and influencing other people. I learned that the world is not interested in your personal strident views, no matter how correct and worthy you may think they are. Young men and maybe women, too, always think that their way is righteous and are not persuaded by argument.

'Politics is about bringing people with you, making decisions as a group for the good of the group as a whole. The English imposed their rule upon us. O'Connell taught us the power of democracy, where all the people are involved in making decisions about the running of the society.

'You must believe in democracy, Ned. It is of vital importance that you, a young energetic man, strive to make Ireland democratic. I know now that you are involved with people that think the way to progress their aims is through force. We will never achieve anything by forcing people against their will. Have not the English taught the Irish that well enough?

'Democracy is the key to our liberation. I mean both Irish liberation and English liberation. Do you think that the ruling class of England care more for their English subjects than their Irish subjects? Not a bit of it, as you can see in this terrible war they are waging. They use their own flesh and blood, Englishmen, as cannon fodder just as wantonly as they use ours. England is divided by a class system, one that did not exist in Ireland until the English forced it upon us. To them everything is hierarchical. Of course, their thinking is false.

'Many English people understand this better than we do in Ireland. For them it is a class struggle, whereas we just lump all the English together as barbarian invaders. But this war has laid bare the truth. The English rulers care nothing for the lives of their own people, and less than naught for ours.'

'Alright, Da, alright.' Ned threw down *The Harness Maker's Guide* and walked out of the shop.

On Sunday, the Volunteers went on a training route march to Ballingeary, 15 miles north of Dunmanway. About twenty of the Dunmanway Volunteers met on the edge of town and Michael McCarthy was in charge.

Michael said, 'We'll follow the road towards Kinrath for a distance, then we'll head cross-country. The object of today's exercise is to familiarise ourselves with the country up to Ballingeary and see how fast we can do it. One day, we may need to get there in a hurry and unseen. So we'll follow the lowest lie of land and keep down by the hedgerows.'

The men started out in single file. Michael sent two men out ahead and two men into the fields to the left and right of the main column as scouts. They carried nothing but canteens of water and some bread stuffed in their pockets. A few of them had hurleys and Michael had an army field compass. He didn't have a map, but had a notebook to write down observations about the route. Wearing flat caps as they always did, they looked as though they were on their way to a hurling match.

About two hours into the trek, the men were walking across fields and up into heather covered hills then back down to more farmland. The column had spread out and Ned was with a group of five of them.

Talking as they walked, they all declared that they were Irish nationalists. But what did it mean to be a nationalist, aside from just saying 'I'm a nationalist'? What were their actual beliefs? What did they hope to gain? Ned was now confronted by these questions. Was he a nationalist or a Boy Scout out on a lark? Could he do what his mother and father wanted, be a nationalist in spirit but take no action?

Everyone seemed to have a different opinion, separate visions. His father was very practical about it. He often said, 'O'Brien and the reforms the Land League forced from the English have transformed Ireland.'

His mother was proud of her husband's achievements in the League. 'Not a shot fired, no punches thrown, all achieved by obeying God's command, love one another,' she sad. 'Don't you forget, Ned. You're a Christian first, a man second and Irish forever.'

His brother Jack had a different approach. 'We have to kick the British out. They will never leave unless we force them out. We have to be prepared to take action. Be ready for the call, Ned.'

Most of the townspeople seemed to have little opinion either way. In any case, they mostly kept quiet about it. 'Walls have ears,' Michael said, 'and they're all Sassenach ears.'

Over the course of a season nearly all the local farmers would come in with harness work, so Tom knew everyone for many miles around. He knew how the crops and livestock were faring and could gauge the mood of the people.

The farmers were taciturn when it came to personal affairs, and politics – talking out of the sides of their mouths with a whisper, half a word. His father knew what they meant and so did Ned, though no outsider would be able to make out a single syllable of what they were saying. This was the product of four hundred years of invaders, landlords and their agents poring over the ancient lands, looking for something to steal, someone to rob.

Entangled in events, Ned could not get free. He was in the Volunteers, he lived in Dunmanway and he couldn't run away. There was nowhere to go, nowhere he wanted to go. He had to decide. Am I in or am I out?

'Well, there is going to be a fight, and we had better be ready for it,' said Michael.

His mother said, 'You must see Ned, we are not divided, we are just one people, English and Irish alike, humans born to suffer and die, with a bit of living in between depending on God's grace.'

In October 1915 another bit of living entered the world. James, the first child of Jack and his wife Margaret, was born.

4

At the beginning of April 1916 Jack said, 'The day is coming soon. There'll be a general action all across the country, including here.'

'When?' asked Ned.

'No date yet, boy, but it will be soon. Con Ahearne has been made Officer in Command of the Dunmanway region. Tomas MacCurtain is the commander of County Cork. Over Easter the Volunteers across the country have been called up for three days of manoeuvres.'

'Is it Easter then, Jack?'

'I wouldn't be able to say, as I'm not IRB, but Con gave me the wink all right. So I think we should be prepared.'

'We could do with more weapons.'

'They're on the way. If Easter it is, then there will be plenty of weapons available when we muster.'

The next day at the Volunteers meeting, a flyer was pinned to the notice board. It was from the leadership of the Irish Volunteers with a message from Patrick Pearse, the Director of Operations. It ordered a general assembly and three days of training and manoeuvres to commence on Easter Sunday.

Easter was late that year, with Easter Sunday falling on 23 April. The weather was warm and dry and spring flowers were in full bloom. In the early evening of Easter Saturday, Jack showed up at the front door of the shop.

Jack said, 'Ned, come let's take a stroll.'

As they walked up West Green towards the town centre, Jack said, 'It's on, all right; we're to muster in Market Square after eight thirty Mass. Get to the square at five to keep watch. A few others will be stationed around town through the night.'

'What about you, Jack?'

'I'm to stay in town and keep watch. I have to back you fellows up, rather than be in the fight.'

Ned went straight to Market Square as soon as he woke before five in the morning. He stood in the shadows, waiting to see who else might show up. The first person to arrive was Jack, who came silently over to where Ned was standing.

A shadow on the other side of the square emerged and orange light sparked as a cigarette was stubbed out on the pavement. The shadow moved towards them, and they soon recognised it was Michael McCarthy.

'It's all right boys, I have security covered. Jack, you go on home. Ned, you stick with me.'

Ned and Michael waited by the square as the sun's rays poked above the buildings and the stars gave way to clear blue sky.

Michael looked at Ned and said, 'I have this for you. Take it.' He took a large revolver, a six chambered Parabellum, out of the inside pocket of his coat, and clinked six rounds of ammunition in Ned's hand. Ned was familiar with the weapon. It was one of three revolvers the Dunmanway Volunteers kept.

'Did any more weapons arrive? Are there any rifles?'

'No, Ned, only what we already have. A ship was bringing more to Kerry, but no sign of it yet. We'll make do, don't worry.'

Ned also had a small haversack with some bread, cheese and eggs to last him a day or so. He had mentioned nothing to his mother, but after supper on Saturday evening she spent several minutes preparing food and wrapping it. She put it in his bag and said, 'This is for tomorrow. Don't eat it all at once, you never know, it may have to last you a few days.'

Thomas hadn't said anything to him until he was about to go to bed. Then he looked Ned in the eye and said, 'Sleep soundly, boy.'

It wasn't until about eight in the morning that other men started to arrive. Soon nearly all the members of the Dunmanway company were on parade except Jack and a few others who would help with communications. After nine o'clock the Behagh and Ballinacarriga units arrived in the square, including the three boys who had confronted Jack, Michael and Ned many years ago. The Lyre unit had marched through the night, attended Mass at St Patrick's and then marched in formation to the square.

Con Ahearne consulted with the officers of the four units, walking briskly between the gathered men. Michael was 1st Lieutenant and in command of the Dunmanway company.

At ten o'clock they marched out of town in formation, north towards Inchigeela. All the men were armed, most with shotguns. Ned kept with Michael, who also had a revolver. A few of the men had rifles and were sent out in front and to the flanks as scouts.

As they marched, Michael shouted out a warning. 'Listen, we must assume that our plans have become known to the Royal Irish Constabulary (RIC) and the army. They might not be so friendly towards us today. We must be prepared for an attack or for them to try to prevent us reaching our destination.'

But, without incident they arrived in Inchigeela soon after noon. As they entered the village, two RIC officers were waiting for them, their arms folded, leaning on a fence. As the column passed them, Con Ahearne touched his cap and said, 'Good morning to you, officers Reilly and McMurrough. A fine day is it not.'

'It is a beautiful Easter Sunday Con, sure it is. Where would you boys be off to today?' said Reilly.

Con just nodded and kept moving. They marched into the town GAA football field where several units from other districts had already formed squares. As they marched past the Brigade Commanding Officer Thomas Mac Curtain, he said, 'Very punctual, men, and in good order. Well done.'

The men formed into ranks and stood to attention. 'At ease, men', said Mac Curtain.

He then drilled them, making them march up and down for several minutes and reviewed the parade. They were then stood at ease and dismissed.

Michael said to the Dunmanway unit, 'Four men keep on watch, the rest of you stand down. We are to reassemble in two hours.'

At about three o'clock they all reassembled, were drilled again, and then dismissed. The companies were ordered to return to their home districts and await further orders.

As they left Inchegeela it started to rain and continued all the way home. Drenched, they reassembled in Market Square in Dunmanway and were finally sent home just before midnight.

As Ned left the square Michael grabbed his forearm and said, 'Another one we missed out on Ned. Keep your powder dry.'

Easter Monday was quiet. Hardly anyone in town ventured out of their houses. Ned was put on nighttime guard duty again in Market Square. Early on Tuesday morning, Michael walked past him shaking his head, 'No word yet, Ned. I'm going to cycle to Ballinadee and see Tom Hales. The only news I have is that the Tricolour is flying over the GPO in Dublin.'

'So it's started!' said Ned

'It's on all right, but I've no orders and no other news. Have a rest now, but keep close. I'll see you around noon, all being well.'

Ned waited nervously at home in the shop, keeping an eye out the door into West Green. About noon he walked the short distance up to Market Square. He passed several other volunteers but they all pretended not to notice each other. Just after two o'clock, Michael cycled into the square and continued on down West Green towards the railway station. Ned knew to follow him. When he reached the junction of Quarry Road he saw Tadgh O'Shea, 2nd Lieutenant, standing on the corner talking to Michael, who was still on his bicycle.

Michael turned to Ned and said, 'Spread the word, we're to stand to until we receive further orders.'

He cycled off and Tadgh turned and walked away. Jack was waiting for Ned on the opposite corner.

'Stand to?' said Ned.

Jack passed him a flyer. Shaking his head, he said. 'I just got this from a train driver down from Dublin. It's the proclamation of the Republic. How can we be stood down while men are dying?'

'Has Michael seen this, Jack?'

'I'm the intelligence officer am I not? I'll bring it over to him now.'

'Is there any other news?'

'The train driver said there's machine gun and artillery fire in the centre of Dublin. Volunteers, Cumann na mBan and Connolly's Irish Citizen Army have occupied the General Post Office, Steven's Green, Boland's Mill, the Four Courts and other places. He says that no more trains are being allowed in or out of the city, and he heard from contacts at Kingstown that troop ships are expected from England any time now.'

'We've got to do something. We can't just sit here waiting for them to come and get us,' said Ned.

Jack also had a newspaper from Dublin. 'Look at this.'

All Irish Volunteers are to stand to, not muster and take no part in any action or manoeuvrers until further orders are issued. Eoin McNeill, Chief of Staff Irish Volunteers

'I'll go see Michael now and get a better picture of the situation.'
Ned walked quickly up the Market Square. He felt that they were all sitting ducks. The English and RIC knew they had marched to Inchegeela under arms. What else had happened around the country, in Cork City? Had everywhere else risen up and was it only West Cork that had failed to act? Or had the towns closer to Dublin seen the order to stand down days earlier, even before the rising had begun? Surely, the British would be on their way to West Cork to round them up, or maybe they are too busy with conflict all over? What a shambles, he thought.

The Volunteers hid on street corners or behind closed curtains. Men were posted on all the roads into town, day and night. On Thursday, a Volunteer from Cork City cycled into Dunmanway to see Michael. He brought the news that Thomas MacCurtain had surrendered the Cork unit's weapons to the army to avoid a bloodbath.

The following Monday, 1 May, a train arrived with printed newspapers from Dublin. After occupying the GPO and other buildings in the centre of Dublin for six days, the Volunteers had been forced to surrender. There were one or two reports of skirmishes in other parts of the country but the rising was now over and a new reality began to sink in.

Ned and half a dozen men left town and stayed in what they hoped was a safe house with one of the McCarthys outside of Dunmanway, and waited for further orders. In the evening, Michael came and told them all to leave their weapons and disperse. 'Ned you stay with me. We need to gather up the weapons and bury them,' he said.

Michael organised several pairs of men to collect all the weapons the volunteers had in their houses or hidden in town and bury them safely in the countryside. 'Spread the word, tell everyone to get away to wherever they can. The army and RIC will raid the town soon, for sure.'

Michael and Ned put their collection of shotguns, rifles, pistols and ammunition in a cart and wheeled them out of Dunmanway after dark, and buried them in a field down by the river.

'We'd better get away now, Ned.'

'I'll meet you on the Inchegeela road in half an hour. I'll go and say goodbye to the family and you do the same.'

Ned walked in the door of the shop in the darkness and tiptoed up the stairs. It was about three o'clock in the morning and both his parents were sitting by the softly glowing turf fire.

'Sit down and have a heat of the tea,' said his mother.

Thomas filled his pipe with tobacco and said, 'You'll be heading into the hills now, I'm sure?'

'I will. I'll go off with Michael. I'll get word to you as soon as it seems safe.'

'Finish your tea and off you go then.'

His mother gave him a haversack full of food and tea. She wrapped her tiny arms around his mud-covered jacket. 'Now remember all the things I've told you Ned. God will light the way for you. Ask and you shall receive, knock and it will be opened up to you.'

The door creaked open and a glimmer of light squeezed out into the darkness as he slipped away. He met Michael, and they trudged up towards Inchegeela and the Cork and Kerry mountains.

They walked north along the road for about five miles to a safe house. It was empty but provisions had been left in case of a situation like this. It was close enough to town that Michael could keep in communication but remote enough to be missed by the army and RIC, or so they hoped.

The next day, 2 May, Ned got up before dawn and set himself up in a copse of trees a few hundred yards from the house. It was best to keep away from buildings as much as practicable in case they were raided. Half asleep, clutching the elbows of his jacket together to keep warm, he heard a squeak, and another. He looked up to see the Dunmanway postman cycling along the road. He knew he would have news and went down to the road to meet him. Michael, who had been watching from the opposite side of the road, arrived at the same time as the postman came abeam the house.

The postman said, 'The RIC arrived in force about an hour ago. I'm doing the rounds to let everyone know. I'll head back south again now,' and off he went.

They spent the rest of the day watching the house and road from a distance. After dark they took shifts, one inside sleeping, while one kept guard outside.

The next afternoon, Jack arrived on a bicycle just before sunset. 'Is it all right, Jack? Can you stay?' Ned asked.

'I've not been followed. Let's go into the house.'

The three men sat around the table, leaning on their elbows, hunched in towards each other. Jack said, 'The RIC searched the town looking for Volunteers. They caught a few of the boys yesterday and today they got Con Ahearne at the safe house west of town.'

'Was anyone hurt?' asked Michael.

'No, but they have also taken Liam Duggan, Tadhg O'Shea, Tim O'Brien, Con Sullivan. Michael, they got your brother Dan.'

'Do you know where they've taken my brother?'

'Cork City, after that I don't know.'

'Oh, by God, I've got to do something to get him.'

'Michael, you've got to move on and lie low. There is nothing you can do for Dan right now. One thing is clear; you and everyone else should hide yourselves deeply for a while. They say that the prisoners who are not being executed will be sent to England.'

'How many do they have?'

'One newspaper said about 1,500 men and Constance Markievicz are being held. Actually, they say about seventy women were captured as well.'

'Have the RIC gone now?'

'Yes, it's now back to the usual Dunmanway detachment and another two they left behind.'

'What's the word from Cork and Dublin?'

'They are reinforcing the garrison in Dublin. A troop ship arrived a few days ago and more are on the way. They are arresting Volunteers all over the country. They have held courts martial in Dublin for the leaders.'

'Who do they have?'

'They captured all the leaders except The O'Rahilly who was killed at the GPO. Pearse, Thomas MacDonagh and Tom Clark were to be shot this morning. More executions will take place soon.'

Jack took the flyer he had shown Ned with the proclamation of the Irish Republic and laid it flat on the table, smoothing it with his fingers. 'Well, in any case they proclaimed the republic. There can be no going back now.'

'Yes, but did people around the country rise up, or was it just Dublin?'

'The word is that most Volunteer units got the order to stand down from Eoin MacNeill and they either didn't muster or went home.'

33

'That bastard,' said Michael.

'Perhaps not, we could have all been killed or arrested. There might have been a shooting war raging right now. We never got the weapons we were promised,' said Ned.

'The guns were on a German boat that was about to come ashore in Bantry Bay when the navy intercepted it,' said Jack.

The men looked at the proclamation and read it over and over to themselves.

POBLACHT NA hÉIREANN
THE PROVISIONAL GOVERNMENT
OF THE

IRISH REPUBLIC
TO THE PEOPLE OF IRELAND

IRISHMEN AND IRSHWOMEN In the name of God and of the dead generations from which she receives her old tradition of nationhood, Ireland, through us, summons her children to her flag and strikes for her freedom.

Having organised and trained her manhood through her secret revolutionary organisation, the Irish Republican Brotherhood, and through her open military organisations, the Irish Volunteers ...

We declare the right of the people of Ireland to the ownership of Ireland and to the unfettered control of Irish destinies, to be sovereign and indefeasible ...

... In every generation the Irish people have asserted their right to national freedom and sovereignty; six times during the past three hundred years they have asserted it in arms. Standing on that fundamental right and again asserting it in arms in the face of the world, we hereby proclaim the Irish Republic as a Sovereign Independent State, and we pledge our lives and the lives of our comrades in arms to the cause of its freedom, of its welfare, and of its exaltation among the nations ...

'Fine words, written by Pearse no doubt. It completely implicates the Volunteers. They will try to round us all up,' said Michael.

Jack stood up, 'I had best get back home.'

'But they'll arrest you, Jack,' said Ned.

'Maybe, but I've a six-month-old baby in the cradle. I wasn't at Inchegeela, they know that. You boys had better move on during the night.'

Jack put several newspapers and some food on the table and left.

The Cork Examiner openly acknowledged that little of 'the truth has filtered through', yet still felt sufficiently confident to describe the insurrection as a 'communistic disturbance rather than a revolutionary movement'. The newspaper exonerated Sinn Féin of responsibility on the basis that armed rebellion was 'out of keeping' with its declared intention to act only in defence.

But the finger of blame was pointed not only at those who had perpetrated the rising, but was scathingly directed at those who had created the precedence for armed resistance in the first place.

> ... Edward Carson, his Ulster Unionist followers and their champions in military and religious life. It was they who sewed the wind and for the moment it looks as if it is we who must reap the whirlwind ...

The majority of the casualties, both killed and wounded, were civilians. Both sides shot civilians deliberately. There were two instances of British troops killing civilians out of revenge. At Portobello Barracks, six men were shot and at North King Street, fifteen were killed.

However, nearly all casualties were caused by fire from artillery, heavy machine guns and incendiary shells. Only the British Army had these weapons and they used them ferociously, turning the buildings around the GPO into burning, bombed-out shells, causing the vast majority of the nearly 1,700 civilian fatalities.

One Royal Irish Regiment officer recalled, 'They regarded, not unreasonably, everyone they saw as an enemy, and fired at anything that moved.'

5

The next morning before dawn, they left the house and continued up the road to Inchegeela. They stayed in a farmhouse outside of the village and moved on a few days later.

'I know a perfect spot up in the hills above the lake at Gougane Barra,' said Michael as they continued towards Kerry. The countryside was dotted with abandoned stone cottages that had been lived in until the famines of the 1840s had greatly reduced the population. With no potatoes, owing to the blight, farmers ate their crops of grain and vegetables that they were due give to the landlord's agents to pay the rent. When they could no longer pay, bailiffs forcibly threw them out of their houses and onto the roads.

Families, grandmothers, mothers with babies, daughters, sons and once-proud fathers were faced with a bleak choice. Stay in the area where they were from and starve, or walk down the road as far as they could before they starved. The strong made it to a town or perhaps a port, and boarded a ship bound for America or England.

Before the famine years, all of West Cork was Irish-speaking. After the famine, when so many people had died or left, it was only in the remote areas and hills around Gougane Bara, Ballingeary and Inchegeela that Irish lived on as the first language.

Gougane Bara, the Rock of Barra, is a tiny island in a mountain lake where St Fionbarr, the patron saint of Cork City, built a monastery in the 6th century. The rocky heather-covered hills are steep and the area remote.

Michael knew of a Seanchaí, storyteller or 'bearer of old lore', who lived there. Seanchaí were the custodians of the Irish oral tradition that had survived through the millennia. They were the last remaining caste from the entwined social structure of Celtic Ireland to have survived the dismantling of the culture.

Michael said, 'We'll go see Colmán Curran and his wife Mary. She's a McCarthy and my second cousin.'

They followed the road west from Ballingeary, along the river Lee. The source of the Lee is the Shehy Mountains and the lake at Gougane Barra. The river winds through West Cork to Cork City where it flows into the sea.

From the river valley floor they headed up into the hills. They reached the crest and looked down into the lake. 'Over there, that's the house, I think. I was only here once a few years ago.'

They continued half-way down the hill to a small dirt road where a whitewashed cottage was nestled into the craggy hill.

As they approached they heard a raucous screech of hens and ducks. A woman dressed in black with a saffron-coloured headscarf came out of the front door with a straw broom in her hand, waving it wildly in the air. 'Out ye now, get back to the yard,' she shouted as hens and ducks flapped and waddled out of the house they seemed to have just invaded.

'Hello Mary, It's your second cousin from Dunmanway,' said Michael with a broad smile.

'Well, that's more of it now, so it is, young Michael, so. Come in and have a heat of the tea.'

The room was effused with afternoon sun rays beaming in the front door, and the flickering glow of a small turf fire in the hearth.

Colmán was sitting on a stool by the fire with a pipe in his mouth and a poker in his hand. 'Well lads, take a seat and warm yourselves by the fire,' he said motioning towards two rickety chairs. Ned and Michael bent down and lowered themselves gingerly onto the seats.

'Sure, it is a fine day, is it not?'

'Sure it is, cousin, it is,' Michael agreed.

Mary brought two mugs from the cupboard and poured steaming black tea from a kettle that was raised on a hook just to one side of the glowing fire.

'You're Michael McCarthy from Dunmanway, if I remember correctly,' said Colmán.

'I am. This is my neighbour and friend Ned. We're just passing by, you know.'

'Ah, just passing. I knew a man once in Cork City. He used to pass by my shop every day. He wanted all the news, the comings and goings. In truth, he was a bit of a strange man always wanting to know everything, but never telling anything of himself,' said Colmán as he tapped the ashes of his pipe into the fire.

He poked and twisted the burning clods of turf and flicked a sod from a neatly formed stack onto the mound of embers. Quickly, it came alight and the heat from the fire increased.

'Well the thing is, Colmán, cousin, we thought we would have a bit of a break from town. You know, before the harvest comes I – we, thought we would go on a bit of a tour of discovery of old Ireland,' said Michael.

'Grand timing, if I might say. Sure, you couldn't have chosen a better time than this to skip town all right. The spring flowers are early this year and blooming in such profusion as I have never seen.' Colmán's eyes lit up with merriment. He pulled a tobacco pouch out from his pocket and filled his clay pipe. 'Do you happen to have any newspapers with you? Being up here we are a bit dependent on people bringing us snippets of news and actual papers are always welcome.'

'We do,' said Michael and he pulled a Cork Examiner from his jacket pocket and gave it to Colmán.

Colmán gazed at the front page with his pipe in his mouth, puffing away.

'Yerra, go on, an uprising in Dublin. How I would love to have been there for that. It would have been interesting to see all the players in that one, for sure. How did they get on?'

He mumbled to himself as he read the account of the seizure of the GPO and the Four Courts, the subsequent artillery barrage and ultimate surrender of the rebels.

'Now, what do you boys think of that, a proclamation of the Irish Republic?'

'Proclamation,' cried Mary from the pantry, 'Well that's more of it now, a proclamation, sure what next? Well, I'm glad they left some of the boys behind to make proclamations, and they didn't all have to go to Germany.'

Mary pushed though the house with her broom blowing dust all around, out into the front yard where soon ducks were quacking and hens flapping as she echoed, 'A proclamation, sure God love us.'

Colmán came to the section that detailed the executions of the leaders of the rising. Since Ned and Michael had left the safe house after seeing Jack, ten more of the leaders had been shot.

'So they shot Pádraig Pearse first and James Connolly while he was tied to a chair unable to walk due to the mortal injuries that he had already received. Why did they waste the bullets? Killing people never solves anything, it only causes complications.'

Colmán put the newspaper down, his hand with pipe curled in his fingers rested on his knee. His soft eyes turned upwards, his face rounded and his voice changed, became deeper and melodious as he began, 'I knew a man once, he was a congenial sort of a fellow, but he had a bit too much of a taste for the drink.

'Well, one night we were in Jimmy Goleen's bar in Cork, it was a grand night with singing and music. Now myself, I like a drink of course, especially in those days gone by. Sure you'd never think of it to look at me, but I've got some years on you young fellows.

'Anyway, Kieran, that was his name, was making merry and downing whiskey as if it was beer. He was just out of the army and full of stories of the boor war. He was very proud to have been a part of it, "fighting for the Queen", and then the King after the Queen had died.

'It is an interesting fact that most people don't seem to know, especially since we are at war with her cousin the Kaiser at the moment, but Queen Victoria was a German. A German you say, Queen of Ireland? Sure go 'way, but it was true.

'Well, at the time of the boor war, at least when it started, she was Queen and young Kieran joined up and went to fight the boors in South Africa. Well, he made it out of that one without so much as a scratch on him, and he was very proud of it.

'That night he had just returned home after years away and he was as joyful as a puppy released from his kennel. He couldn't contain himself, dancing with all the girls and drinking more than any soldier could and still shoot straight, if you know what I mean.

'Well the frivolity increased, as did his amorous advances, until he was caught dallying with a young woman who was merry for the thought of it. She didn't mind a bit. But her husband took exception thinking that they were too close for his comfort. He was right, for a week later the two of them ran away together leaving the poor husband alone and distraught.

'Well, he thought, the only solution was to kill the upstart that was cause of his misery. It took him some time, but he found them together living in a sinful state in Skibbereen.'

'Living in sin they were,' exclaimed Mary as she whooshed through the house, broom in hand, dust flying. 'Skibbereen, oh the shame of it, sinning every day they were.'

Colmán carried on oblivious to Mary's punctuations, 'Well, he killed the blackguard with a schtick. One blow that was all it took. He thought his troubles were over and he would take his darling Jenny back home, but not a bit of it.

'He didn't know it until too late but Kieran's brother was in the RIC stationed in Skibbereen. Not only that, but Jenny didn't want a bar of him. In fact, she was carrying the child of Kieran.

'Chased by the RIC brother, he fled old Skibbereen and went all the way to San Francisco in America and married another woman. He thought his troubles were over until Kieran's other brothers, who had also immigrated to San Francisco, caught wind of where he was living with his new wife and three children.

'Well, Kieran's brothers, as keen as they were at first, didn't kill him, but they might as well have done. For they bled him dry of money through blackmail for years until the poor wretched fellow died of his sorrows, penniless and alone.

'So you would be wise to think hard before you take some vengeful action. It may seem to solve one problem but opens a Pandora's Box of trouble for you.'

Pleased with his moral tale he tapped out his empty pipe and refilled it. Carrying on without interruption of thought he continued, 'Of course, many Irish people emigrated to San Francisco and California, so after a time, a community was there waiting for them when they arrived. But sure, it was a hard life nevertheless. America is a grand majestic nation and not the place for a weak or placid man. Survival of the fittest, or luckiest maybe...'

Ned and Michael slipped into a half slumber, calmed by the tea and caressed by the lilt and rounded timbre of Colmán's rich voice. For a moment they were carried away from their troubles. The tension that had gripped them since Easter seemed to fade away into the past.

Colmán resumed his story, which evolved into a description of life as he imagined it in America. From San Francisco his story travelled across the deserts of Nevada and Arizona, up the Rocky Mountains and down the Mississippi River. He embellished his tale with rich descriptions of places, people, the antics they got up to, the babies they made and the dynasties of Irish emigrants they founded. Piano-like, his musical voice went slow and fast, soft and thunderous. Like a one man band, he made his own accompaniment.

Ned gazed around the cottage taking in the details. It was a one up, one down cottage with a small single story extension. It was one of many such dwellings, built thanks to William O'Brien and the Land League.

After he had helped to usher the Land Act of 1903 into law, O'Brien had pushed the Labourers Act of 1906 through parliament. This provided government funding to construct 'commodious accommodation' on one-acre plots of land with low annuities. Many thousands of these cottages had already been built and more were in construction across Ireland, transforming the countryside.

The main room, with the hearth in the middle of the side wall, had a tiny staircase to the upstairs room. Behind the main room was the pantry, which was Mary's domain. When she wasn't whooshing through the house, sweeping, or on some errand, she sat on a stool in the doorway to the pantry as if guarding it.

The hearth was Colmán's. The large fireplace had a metal crane hung above it in the chimney, with pots and pans hanging down and a big black kettle swinging on a hook. Turf in various stages of preparedness was stacked around it. The closest sod would be added to the fire and the remaining stack would, over time, be shuffled closer until each sod in turn was slipped into place on the fire by one quick tap of Colmán's poker.

The smell of the burning turf permeated the house with a rich loamy odour that conjured up feelings 'as old as the hills'. The scent and smoke brought memories of childhood, of mother with a baby at her breast. Crackling and hissing, it gave up its energy as life-giving heat and light, the remains of an infinity of plants, animals, insects, worms, gestating for countless generations. The ancient vitality of Ireland was compressed there, layer upon layer, not dead but alive, mixing, cooking, reforming. In the pregnant hearth, now ready, its life burst out. It was a physical incarnation of the embrace of Eriu, the soul of Ireland.

Ned was brought back to the present by Colmán's voice, now directed at him.

'What was that, Colmán?'

'I said, there was tell of a bunch of fellows making a merry parade of themselves in Inchegeela over Easter. A fair sight, I heard say. Farmers from all over marched up and down. Then they all went home again. What a strange carry on it sounded.'

Michael, also brought back to earth from his daydreams, pulled himself upright in his chair. 'They may have been the Irish Volunteers, Colmán', he said.

'My mother always said never volunteer for anything. Now you boys wouldn't be so ill-advised as to volunteer, would you?'

'Ah well, Colmán, I don't know. I mean, it is possible.'

'Oh I see. Well I heard that some of those boys decided that they had better keep out of the way for a while after the shenanigans in Dublin, take a trip, maybe a tour of old Ireland.'

'Ah Colmán, you've got us there, fair play. We just think that for a while, maybe we should keep out of sight, you know.'

'I suppose you might be looking for somewhere to rest your bones, somewhere nice and quiet?'

'We would indeed. We had a bit of an idea that there may be somewhere around here, where we wouldn't be in anyone's particular way and we could rejuvenate in the water of the lake.'

'Well, it just so happens there might be a place for you. You see, my son, he went and volunteered and now they've sent him to France.'

'That's a dire shame, cousin. He volunteered for the wrong organisation.'

'Well, anyway, he did it for the pay. He calculated that a year in the army would give him enough money to buy some land. His house is just over the hill. Come, I'll show you where it is.'

Colmán stood up for the first time. He was a well-built man nearly six feet tall. He had a shock of thick black hair greying at the edges and a thick salt and pepper moustache.

He led them out into the yard where Mary was throwing grain down for the hens and ducks. 'Volunteers, sure, what an idea. At least you volunteered to stay in Ireland.'

Colmán walked with them to the crest of the hill and pointed to a craggy outcrop that dropped steeply into the lake.

'The house is just around the other side of the outcrop there. You can reach it by following that path.'

He raised his arm and pointed to a small lightly trodden track that soon disappeared behind the hill.

'You won't be disturbed there at all. If anyone should come this way they will see our house, of course, but you can't see my son's place from the road and only locals know it's there.'

Colmán and Mary loaded them up with milk, bread and potatoes. They took a bag of turf and headed off to their new safe house.

Colmán told them to come by in the evenings as there were often visitors who would sit and talk. Sometimes a fiddler would show up and there would be a nice time to be had. Mary said they could have as many eggs and as much milk as they wanted.

Wild and beautiful, the cottage looked directly over the lake at Gougane Barra. Nestled away in the cottage, they felt a thousand miles from nowhere. The building was solid with three foot thick walls constructed of dry stone, in the same fashion as the boundaries of the fields. Houses were usually stuccoed with a lime plaster, but the render of this house had long gone, indicating that it predated the famine. Nevertheless, with its hard-beaten dirt floor, it was perfectly suitable for Ned and Michael.

It had a hearth and they made a turf fire. They could have cooked for themselves, but instead took most of their meals over at Colmán's and Mary's house. Not only was the food much better than any they could have prepared, but there were always people coming and going, talk and amusement.

Colmán was in his mid fifties and Mary a few years younger. He was from across the border in Kerry, born on the Dingle Peninsula. Mary was from Glandore on the south coast of West Cork.

Colmán and Mary stayed in their 'earthly heaven between the blue sky and the teal green of the lake's water', as Colmán described it. They had little cause to leave as the local people for miles around would, over the period of a few weeks or a month, find some reason to stop by and 'have a heat of the tea'.

Each late afternoon, Ned and Michael would wind their way down the path and around the hill to 'Tír na mBeo', land of the living, as Colmán and Mary called their house, and 'Mag Mell', plain of joy, the one acre of land that the house stood on.

Colmán was full of stories of the past that always combined a moral tale with a caution for the future. Mary was his counterpoint, invariably seeking an ironic twist to Colmán's meanderings.

One evening a musician called Liam came to play. He had a fiddle and Uilleann pipes with him. Michael could play the pipes. Soon the two of them had the audience of Colmán, Mary and several visitors tapping their feet merrily to a jig, then wiping the tears from their eyes as Liam and Michael played soft lilting melodies full of longing and nostalgia.

Two weeks after they had settled into their cottage, late in the afternoon they set off to have their evening meal.

Colmán was sitting on the dry stone wall at the end of the vegetable garden, 'contemplating the mysteries of the cosmos,' while looking out for his one brown cow in the company of his dog, Charlie.

The three men sat on the wall watching the sun go down behind the Shehy Mountains. As the last sun ray dipped below the crest of the hills Colmán said, 'Come inside now. Perhaps tonight we will have a drop of the creature.'

They retired to the rickety chairs nestled in front of the hearth and Colmán flicked two sods on the fire. 'Mary, I think tonight I might have a talk with these two lads. Will you not go fetch the uisce beatha for us?'

Uisce beatha, which Colmán pronounced Ish-key-ba, is the water of life, or as they refer to it in West Cork, the 'creature'. In English it's called whiskey.

'Uisce, is it? That's more of it now. Sure, God love us, uisce, there'll be bells ringing at midnight, and heads ringing in the morning there will.'

Mary scurried into the pantry and rummaged in the half light with shadows dancing off the walls of arms flying, clinking of jars and shifting of boxes, curses under her breath. Finally, she emerged with a bottle of clear liquid in her hand. She took three cups and poured a good measure in each and passed the cups around.

Colmán said, 'Sláinte agus sail agut, ' health and all that goes with it.

Michael responded, 'Taluv gone quis agut,' land without rent to you.

Ned laughed as he chipped in, 'Baan er de vin agut,' a woman to your liking.

They all said together as they clinked their cups, 'Agus bás en Erin,' and death in Ireland.

They took a sip, and although Ned was used to a tipple of poteen, as uisce is also called, this was too strong. He spluttered, 'Colmán, will ye have a bit of water in your uisce?'

'Yerra not at all,' replied Colmán who filed his pipe and puffed as they drank. His eyes, curved in a gentle smile as he regarded his two guests.

The flickering light of the fire captured the gaze of Michael and Ned. The water of life pulsed through their bodies like the smoky breath of a dragon flowing along the meander of a river. The 'creature's' nostrils broke the surface of the water, its eyes flickered green, then dipped again out of sight, its tail flicked from side to side driving the lizard through the liquid in their veins.

Lost in smoky thoughts, Ned tried to imagine a future for himself. In the flames he saw himself making harnesses. But no, scratch that thought. Let's start again. Perhaps I could be a... what could I be? Humm, is there a future after this? His mood turned black, anger crept into him and all he could hear was the hissing of the gas as it was released from the burning turf.

Colmán's voice pierced his consciousness as it had on the first day. At first, it seemed far away, and then it was as if Colmán had prodded him in the guts with his poker. 'So what made you decide to volunteer, Ned?'

'Huh? Oh, well, the cause. I joined for the cause, of course.'

'What cause?' asked Colmán

'The cause of Irish freedom,' Michael piped in.

'Freedom from suffering?'

'Freedom from the English,' said Michael.

'What about you Ned, was it the same for you?'

'Of course, we must be free. Ireland unfree will never be at peace, as Pearse said.'

'It is a funny thing, freedom,' said Colmán, 'I knew a fellow once; he came from a good family. He was well provided for, and he had ne'er a care in the world, if only he knew it. He had money, the love of a good woman, a child and a sporting interest in life. Yet he always felt he lacked freedom. He was never content in himself. One day he decided he'd had enough of this easy life, and he walked away from it all. He left his wife with the baby in her arms and set himself free.

'But what did he do with his freedom? Of course, he went to town and took to the sup. When he ran out of money, the publican threw him out on the street. He was sick as a dog with no money and nowhere to run to, nowhere to hide. In despair, he sat himself at the base of an old oak tree in a field just out of the town.

'There he sat for days on end with only the morning dew that dripped off the leaves of the tree for drink and old acorns which he sucked and chewed as best he could for food.

'He fell into a slumber, a trance, and in his hungered state he began to see the world in stark terms. He realised that all that lives is born to die. Old age, suffering and death of the body is all that any of us have to look forward to. He understood that there is no freedom in this life, and he fell deeper into despair.

'The days wore on and his state changed into indifference. He became detached, neither knowing whether he was awake or asleep, dead or alive. Finally, after many days sitting under the tree, a thought, like a raindrop gently splashing in a pond, touched him. His skin felt a tingling sensation and with a start, he awakened from his distant repose and opened his eyes.

'He saw a young woman, her eyes smiling at him with her hair blown across her face. It was the most beautiful sight he had ever beheld. It was as if an angel from heaven had come to his side. His eyes filled with tears of both joy and sorrow, for he knew he had at last found freedom.

'The girl said, 'Are you not thirsty? Here, take this milk to drink,' and she poured rich creamy milk from a cows horn into his mouth. 'Are you not hungry?' she enquired her head cocked to one side as she placed a spoon of honey in his mouth.

'Well, you are asking, what became of the fellow after that? He married the girl, although he was already married, and fathered seven children with her. He spent his days at the beck and call of his young wife and numerous offspring. For the rest of his long life he never had a moment's peace or any time to himself. He toiled and strived to keep them all clothed and fed and scarce thanks did he ever receive from any members of his family.

'As he lay dying at a ripe old age with grandchildren a-plenty by his side, the priest came to visit him. 'You've no worries now, Brian,' he said. 'You will be free at last in heaven.'

'Yerra, heaven can wait,' said he, 'for I've lived a life of freedom and contentment since the day I became the hen-pecked husband of my second wife. I wish only that I had found out sooner that the less freedom you have, the more free you are.'

Mary slowly picked up the bottle of uisce and poured each of the men a new measure.

Colmán looked Ned in the eye and said, 'What is your name? I mean, your full name?'

'Er, well, my name is Edward Young.'

'Is that all? Did you have no mother, no grandparents?'

'I did, of course.'

'Well, Ned, what are their names, their family names? I mean, where do you come from?'

'Ah, well I'm a Young, O'Brien, O'Connell, Dullea, Connolly.'

'So, you're from around here,' said Colmán nodding. 'From this part of the world, from Ireland, Munster, Cork and Kerry as far back as can be traced. In fact, your family history can be traced much farther back than the King of England. Oh, and he is the King of Ireland as well, of course. Indeed, your people go back yea beyond the Middle Ages, back indeed to the old ancient Ireland of Saint Patrick and further even to the Milesians and beyond more than two thousand years to the Fir Bolug, even.'

'How do you know such things?' said Ned, 'My name means nothing. As to my family history and age, it means less. The country I come from is called The United Kingdom of Great Britain and Ireland. Yet, I don't feel a part of it at all.'

'You only say that because you are unaware of the people who went before you. You feel as though you just arrived here, fresh, new, unique and alone. But of course that's not true. We don't think of horses like that, do we? Every horse is one of a line, a continuation of a family with blood and a track record behind it. We know more about the history of our animals than we do about our own ancestors, the ones from which we came.'

'Maybe that's true Colmán, but so what? I am alive here and now.'

'Then why do you want to fight the English? Surely you could have a much easier life if you just accepted them, fit in with their way of doing things, worked with them in their system.'

'It's not us that have the problem,' said Michael. 'It is they that refuse to accept us as we are, Irish. They have forced their religion, language, culture on us. They want to destroy who we are.'

'So your history does matter, is does define you. Your names mean something after all,' said Colmán.

Michael took a sip of the liquor and said, 'You're right, that's why I decided to fight. I am prepared to die for the cause.'

'Why would you want to die for a cause? Isn't the idea to live for a cause?' said Colmán.

'It's better to die on your feet than live on your knees.'

'Not at all, it's far better to live on your knees than to be dead. The dead can't help anybody; they've gone, leaving us behind. Ireland has seen far too much death. We need young men like you to live.'

'We all have to die sometime,' said Ned

'Yes, but it's God's decision when that time comes. We aren't supposed to help him, give the thing a kick along. We're meant to do the opposite, survive. It is a terrible thing to take a life, either your own or someone else's. It puts you in the place of God.'

Ned said, 'We may not have any choice but to fight. It might be too late. The rising took place and now the English will make reprisals. When someone confronts you, there may be no real choice but to stand your ground. Michael taught me that truth years ago. This is our country; we have nowhere else to go. They can go back to England, but we have to stay here.'

'Well, the real skill of war is to fight on ground of your choosing. They say Napoleon was a genius. His genius was to be so far ahead in his thinking that he outwitted his opponents and forced them onto a battlefield that he had already prepared. Confronting the English in the centre of Dublin was never going to succeed.'

'It's true, at least not militarily. But we also wanted to instill a sense of nationalism in the general population so that they would join the fight. Then the English would be facing the whole country and would have been defeated,' said Michael.

'Every uprising for the last three hundred years has had the same idea in mind. None of them succeeded in rallying the Irish people to their cause, and it didn't succeed this time either,' said Colmán as he turned to push another sod of turf on the fire and refill his pipe.

Ned's answers to Colmán had been disingenuous. He knew all his family history, the names, family lines and where they had come from. Working in the shop and saddlery he had heard the life story of all the families in his part of West Cork.

Michael's family was from the MacCarthy Reagh. They had formed their own kingdom in the Barony of Carbery that Dunmanway was in the middle of. They held their lands and influence right through the Middle Ages. Like all the remaining old Irish families, they were finally dispossessed and destroyed in the Cromwellian war. His family had been in the Dunmanway area for as long as anyone knew, and as Colmán had pointed out, that was confirmed simply by his family name.

Ned's mother was an O'Brien which placed his family in Carbery and Cork as part of the clan of the last great High King of Ireland, Brian Boru, who briefly united Ireland and defeated the Vikings at Dublin in 1014.

Michael's and Ned's people had not migrated from some far off land and settled in Ireland. They were from Carbery, West Cork.

Ned felt this family history as if it chained him to the ground. He was stuck, unable to move.

He longed to be as unfree as the character in Colmán's story. He craved to belong to someone, someone new. Of course, he belonged to his family, his mother and father, brothers, sisters. More than that, he belonged to memory, history, to someone else's dreams, someone else's reality.

His own desire was a love of his own, a woman to give himself to, someone who loved him alone and whom he could love in return. He desired to leave his past behind and re-emerge metamorphosed.

***

Ned and Michael had been living in their little house for nearly four months. They had fallen into a blissful routine and as usual in the late afternoon they walked over to 'Tír na mBeo'. A farmer from Ballingeary was waiting for them. He whispered, 'The word from Dunmanway is that you can come back now, to the safe house, you know.'

They were in no hurry to leave their hermitage. After a few days Michael said, 'Today it is, we've got to get going.' They shouldered their sacks and headed down the road that hugged the banks of the lovely River Lee to Ballingeary and Inchegeelagh and the road to Dunmanway.

The two men walked slowly along the road, lost in their own reveries. It was now August and the river banks were alive with green vegetation, flowers, birds and insects buzzing over the flowing, tinkling stream.

Ned felt peaceful, serene. His feeling and mood was so different from when he had walked up the same road with Michael in May. Then, they had walked quickly, furtively looking back to check that no one was following them. Although Michael would never admit it, they had both been scared, terrified of capture.

They had been intending to take part in an uprising against a heavily armed force, the government of the country, with shotguns, a few rifles and pistols. 'We must have been mad,' muttered Ned.

'What do you mean, Ned, mad?'

'The rising was a suicide mission. We were lucky it was called off.'

'Well, it might not be over yet. We're still Volunteers. I mean, you're still with us, Ned, aren't ye? You weren't persuaded by old Colmán, were you?'

'Of course not, Michael, of course not.'

Ned had loved sitting outside their cottage looking down into the lake at Gougane Barra where St Fionbarr had gone to contemplate God.

At home in Dunmanway he was surrounded by nature. But as a young boy with brothers, the world was always presented as a challenge, a deed to be done, an obstacle to be overcome. Let's see who can run up that hill the fastest, throw a stone the furthest.

At Gougane Barra he had for the first time just sat and contemplated. His recurring dream had been with him the whole time. As he watched the lake he saw his beautiful bride sitting in the boat as he rowed across the water, shimmering in the ever-changing light.

His relationship with Michael had changed. He had known Michael since he was a baby. Michael, too, would sit and stare at the glowing lake, taking out his notebook every so often to write new verses to a song he was writing, quietly singing to himself. Hardly moving for hours they would sit in silence, happy with each other's company. Comfortable, accepting, they felt no pressure to talk.

Day by day the memory of the struggle faded. Dublin, the English and the war seemed an eternity away as if they had never been connected to those things in any way.

But as they headed back down the road, the realisation that the conflict had only just begun and that they still had a role to play in it came back to the men. As they walked, Michael looked over his shoulder and caught Ned's eye. 'We're going back, Ned, back to the fight. It's not over yet.'

Michael picked up the pace and straightened his back. He took on an air of purpose. They were no longer just strolling down a beautiful road.

When they reached the outskirts of Dunmanway, they waited in the fields near the safe house. The next day the postman rode by on his bicycle. They stopped him and sent word to Jack that they were back.

Seán De Siun

6

A few hours later Jack arrived with supplies for them. 'It's great to see you boys looking so well. You look as though you have been at a spa,' he said.

'I'm a changed man alright,' said Ned.

'A lot has changed since you've been in the hills.'

'Is it safe for us to go into town, Jack?'

'You would be welcomed by many people and it will be all right to duck in and out. Unfortunately, the RIC would like to welcome you as well. Most of the Volunteers have scattered, but a few of us are left around the area. The idea is to keep low and look after the hidden arms.'

Ned and Michael moved around West Cork, only staying in one safe house for a week at a time before moving on. The Volunteer numbers had shrunk dramatically to just a handful of active members, all hiding and moving around the countryside. They went into the larger towns regularly, including Dunmanway, but never stayed overnight.

Over the following months, a change occurred in the discourse published in the mosquito and mainstream press. Before the Rising, the portion of the population who called themselves nationalists would settle for nothing less than kicking the English out completely. Another portion of Irish society, however, was doing quite well under the current regime and was completely opposed to Home Rule or any change in the status quo. Why would a person living in successful or privileged circumstances be interested in change?

There were also English settlers and their descendants. Some owned farms, others lived across the country and had businesses, churches, clubs. Many such people felt they were a mixture of Irish and British.

In any case, the two countries were in one United Kingdom, and people wanted to preserve this unity.

In the area centred on Belfast a reasonable majority of the population of four counties, and not far from half the population in two more counties were staunchly British and determined to stay that way.

Across the island, people held a tapestry of opinions, though on an emotional level, many felt a desire for some form of self-government. But when it came to practicalities they were ambivalent. Independence seemed a far away dream that would just never happen and, like most people in history, they were petrified of change.

Ned thought they were scared of change for very good reasons. His reading had taught him that the history of the world is littered with brave and bold actions that end in mass starvation, death and emigration. Going back to ancient Greece, Carthage, Jerusalem and for ever, all around the world, what normally happens when people insist on having their rights or territorial integrity respected is destruction, catastrophe.

Over the period of nearly four hundred years since the Cromwellian war, Irish history had seen a series of disasters. Every seventy years or so there had been an insurrection followed by starvation, death, mass migration, exile and misery. Then the famine years swept away a large portion of the population, its language, its culture and, many said, its heart.

The country was polarised between two distinct groups at either end of a large mass of agnostics or waverers in the middle. But after the Rising and the executions of the leaders, a transformation took place.

The newspapers poured scorn on the response of the government. Ned heard people talking who he knew had spoken against the nationalists earlier on. They were outraged by how the British dealt with the uprising.

An editorial in one newspaper read –

> ... Ireland has sent hundreds of thousands of men to fight and die for the Empire. And the British responded by destroying the centre of Dublin. Without care, they slaughtered hundreds of women and children with artillery and machine guns, and executed wounded men and young boys. ..

Soldiers were everywhere, guns at the ready, staring and threatening. Before the rising they had been, in theory, 'our army'. Now, they were an occupying force.

The irony of a war that Ireland was supposedly fighting to defend 'the small nations of Europe', while it was denied its own nationhood, was impossible to ignore. Yet this was the war that Ireland was fighting. A suppressed yearning for change was given vent.

The transformation was like a cloud forming. No time is involved; it's an instantaneous change of state – one moment, clear sky, the next, cloud. So it was after the Rising. Ireland was different. The old view of the world was history.

Many people at the comfortable extreme did not change their views one bit. Neither did the committed nationalists or northern Unionists. But much of the middle portion of the populace was now with the cause. Like autumn leaves left to dry in the heat of the following summer, fuel will just need a spark to ignite it.

After the Rising was crushed, over three thousand men and seventy women were imprisoned. Many of them had actually not taken part in the Rising at all. Ninety were sentenced to death but in the end only fifteen were executed. Many prisoners were eventually released over the following weeks. But over 1,800 were sent to internment camps in England and Wales including Arthur Griffith, the leader and founder of Sinn Féin. Eamon de Valera was sentenced to death but his sentence was commuted to life imprisonment.

From late summer onward, the interned prisoners were released in batches. By mid 1917 the ranks of the Volunteers began to grow again as the released prisoners returned to Ireland.

Although Sinn Féin was neither republican nor in favour of physical force, disenchantment with the government and Redmond's Irish parliamentary Party led many to abandon Redmond and join Sinn Féin instead. The influx of new members led to a change in the party's position. Under a new broad-based political banner, Sinn Féin changed its manifesto to call for separation from the United Kingdom and an Irish Republic.

In April 1917 the USA joined the war and England was pressured to solve the 'Irish problem'. A general amnesty was issued and the remaining Volunteers, including de Valera, were released. Most of the returned Volunteers joined Sinn Féin and it quickly became the main rallying point of the drive for a republic.

Con Ahearne returned to Dunmanway and was again made the Officer in Command of the Volunteers with Michael his 1st Lieutenant. With the prisoners released, Ned and Michael now felt confident enough to spend more time in Dunmanway. The watchful eyes of the RIC were always on them but no round ups or arrests were taking place.

In the beginning, the Volunteers had been a public declaration to demonstrate that the people were prepared to defend themselves against a militarised Unionist faction. But as time went on it became clear that being associated with the republican movement was likely to lead to arrest or worse. So the Volunteers moved more and more into the background.

Ned was torn between his own desires and the excitement of being caught up in the unfolding drama. He looked back on his time at Gouganne Barra and it seemed a lifetime away. When he joined the Volunteers he hadn't thought the struggle would last so long. He assumed that Home Rule would be enacted and things would change. But now he questioned, how long would he have to suspend his life – the pursuit of the life he desired? At least until the end of the war, that was clear. If he hadn't joined the Volunteers, maybe he would have ended up in the British army one way or another and have been killed in France.

So, no use worrying about it, he thought. He turned his back on his life, mentally locked the door and turned away, focusing instead on the one thing – bringing about the Irish Republic that had been proclaimed.

It was different for Jack. He couldn't turn his back on his life. He already had a wife and his second child had just been born. He stayed in the background, behaving like a good family man and playing the good citizen. He drank in the pubs and said hello to the RIC constables. He no longer showed himself in public as one of the Volunteers.

The IRB had always been a completely secret organisation, and Michael was drawn to them. He understood that this was going to be a real shooting war. The uprising had brought that moment closer. But for now, it was a cat and mouse game. The republicans were the mice and their job was to evade discovery and capture.

It was difficult, nearly impossible, to hide being in the Volunteers as the political situation meant that public support had to be shown for the cause. Jack, Ned and the other Volunteers formed a Sinn Féin club and recruited members, mainly from the families of the volunteers. Through the club they organised music evenings and sporting events as fund-raisers. Ned and Jack's sister Kit and Jack's wife Margaret were founding members of the Dunmanway Cumann na mBan. They promoted civil political affiliation while hiding the fact that they were involved in an armed struggle.

One of the released prisoners was Arthur Ashe from Dingle, Kerry. Ashe was soon re-arrested for sedition after making a speech at a rally. In prison again, he and two other prisoners went on hunger strike demanding to be given the status of prisoners of war. Within weeks he died, and the authorities were accused of torture, force feeding and killing him.

Hunger striking, or fasting on the doorstep of someone who had done you an injustice to bring shame on them, was an old Irish tradition. It was said that even St Patrick used fasting, sitting outside the forts of chieftains, in order to make them convert to Christianity. It was part of the pre-Christian Brehon laws that had survived in Ireland up until the time of Elizabeth I. Allowing a person to suffer or even die on your doorstep for a wrong you had committed would, of course, be an unbearable public dishonour.

Enraged and emboldened by the death of Ashe, the Dunmanway Volunteers decided to hold a public parade in Market Square. As they gathered, the local RIC rushed into the square and grabbed Michael and Con Ahearne. They were imprisoned in Cork City where they too, immediately went on hunger strike until they were released five days later.

In October, 35 year old Eamon de Valera was elected President of Sinn Féin, ousting its founder and leader Arthur Griffith. Sinn Féin was now seen as a young and radical force. Its leaders were young, militant politicians and included Michael Collins from Clonakilty, West Cork, who was just 28 years old.

Events seemed to be moving inexorably towards the republic. 'How could any other outcome now be possible?' said Ned as he and Jack sat drinking pints and reading the newspapers in the Doheny Bar. Jack said, 'Is it possible that the British could be any more incompetent? Every action they take, every utterance they make, drives the Irish people away from them. They are the recruiting engine for the cause of the Irish Republic.'

Irish recruitment to the armed forces peaked in early 1916 and had steadily decreased month by month since then. One reason was the heavy casualties suffered by Irish units in the war. Also, the aftermath of the Rising made it difficult for young men to join the army with the support of their relatives. There was no more waving and singing 'It's a Long Way to Tipperary' as new recruits departed for the front.

In May 1918 almost the entire leadership of Sinn Féin was imprisoned on the pretext that they had conspired with Germany in what became known as 'the German Plot'. They were accused of planning with Germany to open a new front to the war in Ireland. This was dismissed as ridiculous by most commentators and the arrests were generally seen as an excuse to destroy the new Sinn Féin. Held without trial, they were imprisoned in England until May 1919.

After years of costly stalemate, in the Spring Offensive of 1918, German troops broke through the Allied lines across France. The 16th Irish Division held a frontline position at Ronssoy where they suffered more heavy losses and were practically wiped out in the retreat that followed. One battalion was greeted at the rear with cries of 'There go the Sinn Feiners!' Once welcomed as a part of the British war effort, Irish soldiers were now denigrated as subversives and cowards.

Over 6,400 of the men in the 16th division and over 6,100 in the Ulster 36th division were killed. The Irish divisions were so diminished that they were disbanded, and the remaining Irish soldiers were reallocated to other British regiments.

After critical losses over several years, like all the armies in the conflict except the newly arrived Americans, the British were running out of soldiers. Conscription in England, Scotland and Wales – Great Britain – but not Ireland, was already in place. In the spring of 1918 the British Government announced a new 'Military Service Bill' to extend conscription to Ireland. The conscription law was linked to the implementation of Home Rule so that Home Rule would only be implemented if conscription took place.

The IRB and the Volunteers had long said that Home Rule would never happen, that it was a hoax. They maintained that even if it ever was granted, it was too little, far too late. All that Home Rule would do was enshrine into law that Ireland was an integral part of the United Kingdom. It would not grant self-determination to Ireland in any way, but just cement its subjugation to the British forever.

As had been foreseen, Britain had now reengaged on its commitment to Home Rule by cruelly linking it with a 'dual policy' of it only coming into effect if conscription was enforced.

This caused a wave of protest and uproar. At Westminster, the Irish Parliamentary Party and the All-for-Ireland League walked out in protest and returned to Ireland to organise opposition. As a result, the ranks of the Dunmanway Volunteers were suddenly swelled even more.

During the summer of 1918, the Allied forces were strengthened by the Americans, tanks and new tactics, and had finally gained the upper hand in the war. They advanced and forced the Germans back first to the Hindenburg Line, and then further and further into Germany. On 11 November the brutal war finally came to an end.

Across Britain and the Empire, the Armistice on 11 November gave rise to spontaneous celebrations with masses of jubilant people pouring into the streets. In Dublin, there were riots.

Jubilant at first, British soldiers and their supporters celebrated the victory. But their emotions soon turned rancorous. On 13 November, soldiers and a mob rampaged through the centre of Dublin and laid siege to Liberty Hall, Mansion House and the Headquarters of the Sinn Féin party. They carried Union Jack flags, sang Unionist songs, smashed windows and damaged buildings.

Over 200,000 Irishmen had enlisted in the British forces during the war. Approximately 30,000 died plus tens of thousands were wounded. Thousands of men with with appalling injuries were cared for throughout Ireland. These figures do not include Irish emigrants living in Britain who enlisted there, nor the many thousands of Irish born casualties who served in the Australian, Canadian and American armies.

However, unlike other conflicts in Irish history, most notably the Cromwellian war where a quarter of the population is estimated to have died through conflict, deprivation or starvation, there were few civilian deaths.

One newspaper reported –

... Ireland did not suffer the appalling civilian casualties that the direct combatant countries such as Belgium suffered. Unlike the other small nations of Europe it was only our brave men who volunteered to serve who paid the ultimate cost for the cause of civilisation ...

Ireland was not yet one of the small nations of Europe, but Ned, like his brother Jack, his extended family, much of the population of Dunmanway, West Cork and much of the rest of Ireland, were more determined than before to make it one.

The victorious allies, led by the Americans, announced that there would be a post-war peace conference at Versailles in France commencing in January 1919. American President Woodrow Wilson had issued his Fourteen Points policy, which promised that self-government and self-determination would become normal policy in international relations. Sinn Féin's policy demanded Irish representation and recognition at the peace conference. In contrast, the Irish Parliamentary Party's policy was to leave the negotiations to the British government.

As Jack and Ned bided their time, it was becoming clear that the Irish Parliamentary Party, after representing Ireland in Westminster for decades, had lost much of its support. Home Rule now seemed an idea from another era. No one was interested in its enactment except the British Government, who appeared to be oblivious to the changes that had taken place in Ireland.

The war drew to its conclusion and the United Kingdom prepared for its first General Election since 1910. As was the case throughout the United Kingdom, there had been a dramatic generational change in Ireland during the war years.

Because the 1915 election had been postponed due to the war, men between the ages of 21 and 29 were getting their first chance to vote. Also, for over a hundred years, large numbers of young Irish people had emigrated to America, Canada, Australia and other countries as they reached maturity. However, while the war was raging, leaving had not been possible. Consequently, large numbers of young men who would have left Ireland instead remained, and now they had the vote. No one could tell how they would cast their ballots.

The British electoral system had also evolved and for the first time, women over 30 years old, as well as all men over 21 and military servicemen over 19, were given a vote without having to have property qualifications. These changes increased the Irish electorate from roughly 700,000 to nearly two million. These unprecedented advances in democratic representation had profound implications.

The Irish Parliamentary Party had been the majority party in Ireland for forty years but they never had their aspirations fulfilled. Home Rule had been thwarted time and again. But now the Irish people were about to express their political will once more and Sinn Féin would be their new voice – except for the Unionists.

Although dozens of Sinn Féin candidates were either in gaol or in hiding, their names were still included on the ballot. While the rest of the United Kingdom fought the 'Khaki election', in Ireland it was the 'Republican Election'.

Ned, Jack and Michael were suddenly busy. Jack burst into the Doheny Bar and declared, 'This is it, we're finally going to get the Republic. But first we have to win the election. We've been given protection duty for Sinn Féin. We're to make sure the RIC don't disrupt any rallies they hold in town. Michael Collins is coming next week.'

Collins was the candidate for Cork South. As no other candidates were running, his election was assured. Nevertheless he campaigned, making speeches in towns around the county. But the RIC were determined to arrest him.

When Collins came to Dunmanway, Ned, Michael and the Volunteers positioned themselves around the town so as not to draw the attention of the RIC. It was Saturday and Market Square was full of people from the surrounding area. Two RIC lorries and many constables stood menacingly by their vehicles, batons in hand.

Ned and Michael were standing inside the Shamrock Bar on the square. Jack found them and said, 'Collins is going to be at the playing fields on Quarry Road, pass the word.'

As the news was passed from person to person around town, Market Square began to thin out. Eventually the RIC noticed that they were in the wrong place. They jumped in their vehicles and drove around town until they found a crowd of tightly packed people around a table in the middle of the pitch. Michael Collins was giving forth, shaking his arms and waving his fist in the air.

The Volunteers had formed a circle around the table, guarding Collins and holding hurleys. Ned was in the front line and watched through the crowd as the RIC lorries arrived. The constables formed a group and pushed their way through the crowd, punching their batons out in front of them and forcing the people to disperse.

The police edged closer and closer to the centre as the crowd shouted in protest. Ned and the other Volunteers fended them off and pushed back. The RIC were surrounded by the angry crowd in a scrum pushing back and forth against each other, batons and hurleys flailing.

Collins jumped off the table and with his men slipped through the back of the crowd. They crossed Chapel Street and ran into the house of the Curate Fr Carmody near the church. They moved into the fields out the back of the house and disappeared into the countryside. The RIC, having missed their quarry, pulled back and drove away again to their barracks.

The election took place on 14 December and when the votes were counted, Sinn Féin had won 70 percent of all seats in Ireland. However, they won 91 percent of the seats outside of the Unionist areas around Belfast where the Irish Unionist party took 22 seats with three other seats going to small unionist parties. The Irish Parliamentary Party was reduced to just six seats.

The uncomfortable reality, held in denial by much of the population outside of the Unionist areas, was that the country was split, with most of the island wanting a republic, but the counties centred on Belfast determined to stay part of the United Kingdom.

Sinn Féin's policy was that their elected members would not take their places in the UK Parliament at Westminster, but instead set up an Irish Parliament in Dublin named Dáil Éireann, the Assembly of Ireland. The First Dáil met on 21 January 1919.

Sinn Féin was the only party there. All the other elected Members of Parliament including Unionists were invited but declined. Thirty three elected Sinn Féin members were unable to attend as they were in prison.

The First Dáil issued a 'Declaration of Independence', ratified the Proclamation of the Irish Republic that was made in 1916, and declared itself to be the parliament of this new state. They issued a 'Message to the Free Nations of the World', which stated –

> ... Ireland to-day reasserts her historic nationhood the more confidently before the new world emerging from the war, because she believes in freedom and justice as the fundamental principles of international law; because she believes in a frank co-operation between the peoples for equal rights against the vested privileges of ancient tyrannies; because the permanent peace of Europe can never be secured by perpetuating military dominion for the profit of empire but only by establishing the control of government in every land

> upon the basis of the free will of a free people, and the existing state of war, between Ireland and England, can never be ended until Ireland is definitely evacuated by the armed forces of England ...

However, none of the free Nations of the World recognised the new Republic, and the newly self-declared government carried on in isolation.

On the same day, two members of the RIC were ambushed and killed by Volunteers at Soloheadbeg, Tipperary. Although the Volunteers took this action on their own initiative with no authorisation from the new Dáil, the ambush was seen as an act of war and the Volunteers were soon known as the Army of the Irish Republic. So began the Irish War of Independence.

Seán De Siun

7

1919 passed like a shadow war. 'Are we ever going to see any action?' Ned asked Jack as he sat down across from him at the kitchen table at his brother's home. Jack was reading a newspaper with his two arms holding the pages open. His face was completely obscured by the large paper but Ned could see the masthead, *The Irish Times*, and read the main headline - *No Recognition*. The British government declared that they did not recognise the Dáil. 'No surprise there,' said Jack from behind the paper, a puff of smoke billowing out around the edges as he exhaled his cigarette.

In September 1919 the Dáil was finally declared illegal and from then on was only able to meet in secret. Just one month before, in August 1919, the Volunteers formally changed their name to the Irish Republican Army (IRA) and swore an oath of allegiance to both the Republic and the Dáil.

Whom did the new army serve? Was it the elected parliament of the people, or of the nation called the Irish Republic? For now, the Dáil and the Republic were considered one and the same, and Ned and all the other Volunteers in Dunmanway solemnly swore the oath of allegiance.

After taking the oath, Ned, Jack and Michael went in the back door of the Doheny Bar.

'Well, I swore an oath to the Republic anyway,' said Michael slamming his empty whisky glass on the bar.

'I swore allegiance to uphold the democratic will of the people of Ireland as expressed in their legitimate election of members of the Dáil Éireann and the Irish Republic,' bellowed Jack as he slammed his empty whisky glass down with twice the thunder of Michael.

'I don't know myself, but I'm there for the Republic all the way,' said Ned as he downed his Paddy, carefully placing his glass on the bar when he had finished.

The Dáil carried on without regard for the British, setting up a parallel government at the same time as undermining the existing regime, by simply ignoring it into history.

The Dáil legislated to set up courts, appointed judges, authorised tax collection and established the apparatus and civil service of a modern nation state. The Cumann na mBan, with members already in place across the country, were essential in establishing and running the Dáil Courts and local authorities.

The Dáil ordered that the British administration be boycotted and ignored. They declared that any judgement or ruling made by the old regime was illegitimate and that only the Dáil's orders were legal and enforceable.

In response, the British increased their use of force. Reluctant to send the regular army into Ireland in greater numbers, a reserve force of the RIC was created to maintain control and fight the IRA. Newspapers carried advertisements seeking men willing to face

> ... a *rough and dangerous task* helping the RIC to police an *increasingly anti-British Ireland* ...

In early 1920 the new force was deployed in County Dublin, Munster and eastern Connacht. They were British Army veterans of the Great War. Most of the recruits came from Great Britain, but Irish veterans and ex-British soldiers living in Ireland joined as well. Officially they were not soldiers but 'Temporary Constables' under the ultimate command of the RIC, but in reality they had their own commanders who worked closely with the British Army. Initially they were to be outfitted in RIC policeman's uniforms, but due to the sudden influx of new 'constables' there were not enough to go around. As a result, they wore a mixture of dark blue policeman's jackets, khaki army trousers and assorted belts and hats.

In March 1920 the Limerick Echo wrote about a group of the new constables, commenting that their attire was like the Scarteen, County Limerick, fox hunting Beagles whose coat pattern gave the hunt its nickname, the 'Black and Tans', or 'Tans'. This moniker for the new force spread as quickly as their notoriety for drunkenness, ill-discipline and brutality. The remark that they were paid 'ten shillings a day to murder the Irish people' was heard in the shops and pubs in Dunmanway.

One by one, Volunteers were caught by the RIC and Tans. Ned heard from Jack that Michael had been arrested. 'We may never see him again', said Jack. A few weeks later news arrived that Michael was part of a hunger strike by prisoners in England.

Ned felt resigned to his fate. It's only a matter of time before they get me, too, he thought. Will I have the strength go on hunger strike? Forced to spend more time in hiding, afraid to show himself anywhere, dread fear of isolation gripped him as he hid in a farmer's barn. I'm not really alone, he told himself. I'm still part of an organisation, just a shrinking one. But Jack and Ned stayed in contact, meeting every week at a farm somewhere in the district.

Then in June, Michael was back. He was unwell and was being cared for by his McCarthy cousins on a farm near town. Ned found his way over to see his friend, and he recounted the details of his ordeal. He had been first sent to gaol in Belfast. 'There were loads of us in the prison and we smashed the place up as best we could. So they sent me and some of the others to Wormwood Scrubs in London. We went on hunger strike for eighteen days. They said there was to be general release and kicked us out, so I'm back,' said Michael.

Michael acted as confidently as he always did, but he had lost a lot of weight and looked pale and sick. His dark hair had thinned out and his already angular face looked gaunt. His usual healthy country complexion had turned ashen grey.

'You aren't looking too good boy', said Ned.

'Neither are you Ned, but we better keep strong. We aren't finished yet.'

In July 1920 the British sent the 'Auxiliary Division' of the RIC. The Auxiliaries, or Auxies, recruited only British Army and Air Force officers – lieutenants, captains, majors and colonels. The Division's role was to conduct counter-insurgency operations against the IRA. They were paid £7 per week, twice what a Tan was paid. They were officially 'temporary cadets'.

Like the Tans, the Auxiliaries were nominally part of the RIC, but actually operated independently, divided into companies, each about one hundred strong. They were heavily armed and mobile. Roaring into villages in Crossley Tender lorries, they would pour out, assault men and women, destroy property and shops and create havoc. They operated in ten counties, mostly in Munster, and were particularly active in County Cork. They wore either RIC uniforms or their old army uniforms along with distinctive Tam o' Shanter caps. They were commanded by Brigadier-General Frank Percy Crozier, a former officer of the Unionist paramilitary group, the Ulster Volunteer Force.

Jack said, 'They are so brazen as to put a UVF man at the head of the force sent to oppress us? If there were any need of further proof that the creation of the UVF was coordinated by the British Army, we now have it.'

In June, 2,000 additional regular British Army troops landed at Bantry, increasing the feeling that the country was occupied by a foreign force. In response, the IRA ordered all brigades around the country to set up Flying Columns – small independent military units capable of rapid movement and armed with what they had to hand. They were to strike the British at any time and place that they saw fit.

The RIC had many reinforced barracks throughout West Cork and several were attacked and burned down. Soon the RIC needed to consolidate their forces and many of their barracks were abandoned, leaving much of the area without police. One day they suddenly evacuated their barracks at Ballygurteen just south of Dunmanway. A few days later Ned and the Dunmanway Company, or column as they now referred to it, burned the barracks to the ground.

The column now met only at night in remote farm houses away from town. They split up into small groups and cut bridges and roads, isolating areas to make them difficult for the British and RIC to enter.

The column had never had enough arms, but with the increased membership they needed even more. The problem was not lack of funds but the fact that firearms were difficult to source. One night Michael and Ned broke in through the back door of a gun dealership in Dunmanway that sold shotguns and small bore rifles for hunting. They were able to take some shotgun shells but no firearms.

In early August 1920, Michael and Ned met at the McSweeney farm. Michael said, 'There's a Tan in town on his own, standing near the square. I don't know why they left him on his own, but quick, let's go get his rifle.'

The soldier looked bored, standing guard and watching the market square. As the two of them walked past him, Michael pushed a revolver in his face while Ned grabbed his 303 rifle. He dropped to his knees and raised his hands. Ned took his ammunition belt and the two men ran up the street and out of town. In the days that followed there were rumours that the Tans were going to raid Dunmanway in reprisal, but they didn't.

During the summer of 1920, the Tans burned and sacked numerous small towns throughout Ireland, including Balbriggan, Trim, Templemore and others. Martial law was declared in many areas of the country including West Cork.

Tans drove around the countryside and towns in lorries. They took hostages and placed them as human shields in the front of their vehicles. One day the postman cycled past the safe house where Ned was hiding. As usual, Ned went out to see if there was any news. The postman had a terrible scowl to his face as he whispered to Ned, 'Boy, they've arrested your father and are keeping him in the Dunmaway barracks. They're after you. They have a notion that you supplied guns for an operation. Anyway, they're driving around town with Tom handcuffed in the front of their lorry.'

Ned was enraged. 'I'll never forgive them for this.' he said. 'He's an old man and they've taken him hostage, hoping we'll use him for target practice.'

The Volunteers had now been meeting regularly for years. Yet they still lacked any formal military training. While in internment some prisoners had been schooled in war tactics and basic training by the experienced soldiers among them. The Volunteers were now also joined by returning soldiers from the war, and they began military training in earnest in the countryside around West Cork. A series of week long training camps were organised, led by principal trainer, Tom Barry.

Tom was born in Killorgin, Kerry. In 1915, aged seventeen, he enlisted in the British army. He was trained and sent to Mesopotamia where he was involved in much military action. He was discharged in 1919 and returned to Ireland. It was only then, having been thrust into the cauldron of Ireland's political turmoil, that he joined the West Cork brigade. He soon established himself as a valuable asset, introducing British military training and tactics to the IRA.

In September Michael and Ned walked south to a farm in the hills between Killbrittain and Bandon for a week-long training course. Other men from brigades around West Cork also made their way there in ones or twos, taking different routes to avoid the Tans. After finding a place to put their gear and sleep in the farm's barn they fell in outside with the rest of the thirty-five men on the course.

Soon Tom Barry marched up. He was a wiry fellow with a shock of black hair and had a determined grimace on his face that made him look as hard as nails. His fists were clenched and his teeth held shut tight. At any moment you would expect an explosive punch to come flying out at you. But then someone asked him a question and a broad grin appeared on his face in a flash. 'All right, we'll get to that soon enough,' he said. But then his determined grimace returned.

He proceeded to give a lecture on defence and security of the column. He told them that from now on they were to assume that the British could find them at any moment and attack. Their lives were now full time on guard, watching for any sign, suspicious of everything, ready to leap to armed action.

For the next week they were trained in guerilla warfare. They learned how to move silently and swiftly and take firing positions for defence or attack. Day and night they trained, practised manoeuvres and were given lectures on tactics and communication.

At the end of the week the men were dispersed. The Dunmanway group went home and spent the next weeks passing on all they had learned to the rest of the brigade. Over one hundred and fifty men in the West Cork area were trained by Tom Barry.

In mid-October, Con Ahearn and Michael organised an attack on the Dunmanway RIC barracks. Armed with shotguns and two rifles, ten men surrounded the garrison and fired their weapons at the building. One RIC officer was wounded, but they returned fire. Soon the men disappeared back into the night. The next day intensive raids were carried out in Dunmanway by Tans and Auxies.

Jack stayed at home with the curtains drawn. At about three in the morning, he heard the sound of rifle butts bashing on the front door and Tans shouting, 'Open the bloody door, quick.' Jack dashed out the back door and proceeded down the garden. He saw two soldiers moving quickly in the back gate of the house next door and run up the garden. He froze still until they passed him. He looked over his shoulder. They've gone to the wrong house, thank God, he thought, continuing out the back gate and into the night.

Ned moved back out into the country towards Inchigeelagh and stayed in a safe house in the hills. Michael went south towards Glandore.

The British had arrested many Volunteers as well as politicians and other people they suspected of supporting the Republic. The Mayor of Cork, Terence MacSwiney, had been arrested and sent to gaol in England. He died on hunger strike in Brixton Prison in October.

Then, dramatically, on 21 November the IRA Director of Intelligence and architect of the guerilla war, Michael Collins, led a series of attacks in Dublin that largely wiped out the leading British intelligence operatives in the capital. His squad shot 19 people, killing 14 British army officers, police officers and several members of the undercover British intelligence unit known as the 'Cairo Gang'.

In response, Auxillaries and RIC drove lorries into Croke Park, Dublin's GAA football and hurling ground, during a match, shooting at random into the crowd. Fourteen people were killed, including one of the players, and a further 60 people were wounded. Later that day two republican prisoners and another man who had been arrested with them were killed in Dublin Castle. The official account was that the three men were shot 'while trying to escape', but most people believed that the men had been tortured and murdered. This day became known as Bloody Sunday.

The next day Ned met Michael at a safe house outside Dunmanway. Michael said, 'An action is being planned. We're to head to Togher straight away.'

8

Ned was brought back to the present by an elbow in the side from his son Johnny. The funeral Mass was over and Tom's casket was placed on the shoulders of six men and carried from the church.

The last time he had seen Tom alive was during the Anniversary Commemoration at the Kilmichael memorial. Strange how things work out, Ned thought. Here I am, eighty-eight years old. Jack is dead, Collins, de Valera, now Tom. Most of them, the Volunteers, are dead. Nearly all the boys who were at Kilmichael that day, including Tom, of course, are gone now. At least we got the Republic in the end. It felt so close but maybe Collins was right, we were never going to get all we wanted. Only three and one third green fields ended up in the Republic.

His heart still felt wounded, as if a part of it was missing as he recalled the years of his life taken by the struggle. He sat still in his pew as people, one by one, stood and shuffled out. Lost in his memories, thoughts flooded his consciousness. My life didn't unfold the way I wished, in those years anyway. I wanted a peaceful life, and to be left alone to pursue my dream. Who knows how or why things happen? Did human agency really have anything to do with it, or was it fate or some guiding spirit that made events take place the way they did?

He remembered when he was a boy being sent to school for the first time. He had cried to his mother, 'Ma I don't want to go to school!' But she scolded him, 'Never mind what you want, think what God desires for you. It's only through the love, the grace of God, that you are here at all.'

But what God would have desired me to do what I did? Maybe it was Ériu or Queen Maeve who invited me to walk with her into battle. All I wanted then was to fall in love and marry. Instead, another door was opened for me and I shed blood to redeem the nation. Still, we got a memorial. Lest we forget, as they say. They shall be remembered forever, alive forever, speaking forever and heard forever. But everyone will forget eventually. Why not, after all? As the world meanders through time, history matters less and less until the old stories become the source of myths, collective memory, echoes reverberating in the lilt of a melancholic tune.

He remembered when it all came to a halt. Suddenly there was a truce – no fighting, at least for a while, and we had to bide our time again and await the outcome. When the treaty was being debated, Jack said, 'A deal is on the table and we should take it. We won't get everything we want – not now, not in one go.'

But that was not acceptable, he thought, not for me, for de Valera or Tom. We were convinced we would get everything. All or nothing – the Republic for all Ireland or we would keep fighting forever, like the Fianna. It worked out in the end, I suppose. Things did not fall apart. The nation was built and progressed. After all, we managed to keep out of the Second World War, unlike the slaughter in the first one. Ireland and the Army of the Republic did get peace for the most part – no wars, just peacekeeping roles with the UN. Peacekeepers are what the Irish Army turned into – perfect.

Ah, he remembered, but the civil war wasn't peaceful at all. It was far worse than the Tan war. Back then, we had the support of the people and by the end they thought we were great, that we had succeeded and won freedom for Ireland. But in the civil war we lost so much – family, friends, trust and love. I was so young then but felt so old. I feel much younger now.

When it was all over, when I was able to return home to Dunmanway my health was ruined. I remember that Jack and his wife sent over their young son to watch out for me while I recovered. 'Pat me on the head, will ya Uncle Ned?' little Fachtna would say.

If only the dead, the ones we lost, could have lived to see it. Perhaps they can. They might be close by, looking down on us all. Or maybe it's just imagination. Perhaps they can't see us and we can never reach them. They have left this place and are now outside time, across the thin line of existence. The whole circle can never be seen, only felt, believed. Tom is with them now, with Michael and all the others in Tír Tairngire, the Promised Land.

He remembered a story Colmán had told him and Michael when they were at Gougane Barra so many years before.

'There was a young man who had so great a desire he could almost feel it, smell and touch it. He sat at the kitchen table with a strange look on his face as if he were in a trance. Fionn, his mother shouted at him, wake up and eat your dinner. What a dreamer you are, you spend most of your life in some other world.

'Young Fionn was brought back again by his mother's voice but he could never shake the painting-like vision he had created in his mind. He saw his wife, a beautiful black haired girl sitting by the turf fire with his baby in her arms. He was standing by her side, a gold watch in his waistcoat, a pipe in his mouth and a smile on his face, for he had all he desired. The love of a woman, a son, a house, land and a cow with no rent to pay.

'But poor Fionn was never able to make his dream come true. He struggled for years to save enough to buy some land. But any money he ever earned slipped through his fingers like water in a stream. He was an attractive fellow, in the eyes of women, that is, and he had no shortage of beautiful young coleens that took a fancy to him. But he never paid attention to any of them, for they all had blonde or brown hair, and the girl he desired would have dark, black hair.

'He travelled all over Ireland courting every black-haired girl he could find but none of them returned his affection. Perhaps they could sense that he was in love with his dream and had no real care for them.

'After many years of searching and striving, desperate, he cried out, "God in heaven, I give up. You tell me what you want me to do for I've failed at everything, and never gained anything that I desired."

'Well, soon after that he found employment in a shop in Kilkenny. One day a woman with the longest flaming red hair he ever did see walked in, and didn't he fall in love with her on the spot? She had a baby girl in her arms and two more infant girls pulling at her skirts. She was a widow and had no money at all.

'Even so, he married her and they lived in a small rented house in town with a coal fire and not enough room for a cat let alone a cow. They never had any children together, but he did his best he could to bring up his step daughters and was a caring father to them. Resigned to his fate, he spent the rest of his days contented. It wasn't what I wanted, he said to himself each night as he went to bed. I'm not sure whose dream it is, but someone's desire is being fulfilled.'

The congregation in the packed church followed the casket out and Johnny finally brought Ned back from his thoughts, 'Come on now old, man,' said Johnny and he ushered him into a car. Ned sat in the middle with his son on his left and his wife on his right. He thought, it took a few years, but in the end I did get my desire, my girl in the boat and my three sons and beautiful daughter. Love covers a multitude of sins.

On the way to St Finbarr's Cemetery where Tom was to be laid to rest, Ned was transported once more back to Kilmichael.

9

Ned and Michael made their way cross-country to Togher north of Dunmanway. Tom was there to greet them as they arrived. Volunteers arrived alone or in small groups from all around the area. When the column was complete, they were divided into three sections with commanders appointed to each one. Michael was put in charge of Section 2, which included Ned.

Tom said, 'There will be an ambush in a few days. I will let you know more in due course. We'll keep on the move to our objective. First, we'll go to a house at Aghilane near Ballineen and billet there.'

The three sections moved separately cross-country. Unarmed scouts were sent out ahead to make sure the way was clear and they took care at every road crossing. By that night they converged on the farm at Aghilane. Guards were posted all around the farm and the men took turns at sleeping.

On Friday Tom and Michael took two horses and left before dawn to decide on the exact location for the ambush. They arrived back in the late afternoon. After eating dinner Michael and Ned went outside for a cigarette. 'We found a good spot, Ned. Get some sleep, we're to set off early Sunday morning.'

Later in the evening all but two men who were left on guard, gathered to say the Rosary. They knelt on the floor of the barn and one man led them in prayer …. Hail Mary full of Grace, the Lord is with thee...

In meditation, each man lost in his own reverie, but together as one, they said the five decades of the Rosary. As they recited the prayers, Ned could think of nothing but the small figure of his mother kneeling on a chair turned backwards, gathered with the rest of his family to say the Rosary as they always did on Sunday afternoons.

On Saturday evening, Canon O'Connell, the Parish Priest of Ballineen, arrived and waited by the hedge outside the farm gate. One by one the men went out and he heard their confessions. When he had finished he came into the farm and wished them luck and said, 'Be careful, you're in the middle of the Sassenachs. God keep you all. Now I will give you my blessing.' The men all bowed their heads as he made the sign of the cross, then mounted his horse and rode away.

Ned slept alongside two other men fully clothed, lying sideways across the bed so that they could all fit with their booted feet dangling over the edge.

Just before 2am, 28 November 1920, Michael came in and yanked the men awake by their ankles. As if they had not really been sleeping at all, they jumped up, picked up their rifles and fell in outside with the other men in the dark wet night. Tom walked along the ranks and patted several of them on the shoulder as he passed.

Every man had a rifle and 35 rounds of ammunition. Some extra shotguns were slung over the shoulders of a few of them, and one of the men in Tom's Section had hand grenades strapped to his belt.

Tom said, 'We're moving out and we'll ambush a detachment of Auxiliaries in the morning.'

They walked cross-country in continuous drizzling rain. 'Perfect weather for our purposes,' said Michael with a smile. No one said where they were going, but Ned could tell that they were headed towards Macroom. As the first grey tinge was creeping out of the darkness in the east, they arrived at the ambush site.

They were on the road to Dunmanway, near the village of Kilmichael about seven miles from Macroom. Ned looked at his watch as the minute hand clicked to 8am.

As the weak sun shed light on the terrain, clumps of rocks covered in heather and gorse emerged through the gloom at various points along the road. To the North was a farm house on the edge of a low-lying boggy field. It was at a spot where the road from the North turned east for about 150 yards before turning south again. It was typical terrain for this part of West Cork, and Ned was familiar with this stretch of road. He had been through the village of Kilmichael several times, walking the road as he and Jack often did between the towns and villages surrounding the hub of Dunmanway.

Tom said, 'Two lorries of Auxiliaries typically make forays out from Macroom along this road. We expect about ten heavily armed soldiers in each one. But we can't be sure that there won't be three or even more lorries in the convoy.'

Tom and Michael showed the three Sections where to take up their positions. Tom and a dozen other men were positioned north of the road at the eastern end, behind two fences of a lane and two low rocky outcrops.

Six men were scattered into the undergrowth on the south side of the road opposite Tom's command position. Their job was to prevent the Auxiliaries from escaping the fire from Tom's Section and taking up positions on the southern side of the road.

Six other men were sent around the bend from where the lorries would come and took up positions on higher ground there, as insurance in case more than two vehicles were in the convoy.

Ned and Section 2 were positioned north of the road 150 yards further west towards Macroom. By 9am they were in place and the trap was set.

Michael said, 'Ned, you cross the road and take up a position there. The boys from Section 1 haven't got that spot covered. Soldiers from the second lorry might make a break down the lane or over to the farmhouse.'

'Right, Michael,'

Ned found a good spot about 50 yards from Section 2, across the road behind some rocks at the edge of the boggy ground that led to the farmhouse. From his position he could see up the road towards Macroom from where the Auxiliaries were expected to come, as well as down the road to where Tom Barry and Section 1 were positioned. Looking across the road he could see his friend Michael, Paddy Desay and Jim O'Sullivan. Michael nodded at him and Ned waved back. Then a long and boring wait ensued.

He nestled himself in behind the gorse, the tiny faded yellow buds still clinging to the rough shrub in the chill November air. There were few insects, no birds, just still cold air and dim sunlight. The smell of cow manure filled his nostrils. Ned waited, settling his 303 rifle in his arms. He found himself singing, his mind drifting.

Just before 4pm Tom visited him. 'How are you Ned? Keep alert. They will either come this way soon or they won't come today,' he said.

'I'm grand,' said Ned. 'I'm used to waiting, always waiting.' He smiled at Tom, who in a flash jumped up. 'They're coming,' he said.

Ned looked towards the scouts and the farthest one was waving his signal. But then a horse came around the bend, pulling a motorcycle sidecar loaded with five armed men. Ned recognised them as Volunteers who were supposed to meet the column back at Tohgher.

'God almighty,' muttered Tom, and he ran out into the road and waved the horse and sidecar to turn right and head up the lane beside Ned's position. 'The Auxies are coming. Gallop up the lane, get out of sight, gallop, gallop!' Just as they pulled out of sight behind the hedge, the first Crossley Tender lorry came into Ned's view.

Tom shouted for all the men to hear, 'Lie flat and heads down until firing commences.'

Keeping low he ran back along the road, his green tunic flapping. He stopped for a moment and turned back to Ned and motioned with his head up the road to Macroom. Ned turned to look and now saw two lorries speeding towards him, and he dared not move lest they see him.

The sun was low in the southwest, casting a dim shadow over the vehicles, but he could see the points of rifles sticking up. He didn't move. If they haven't seen me, they won't if I just keep still, he thought. The driver of the first lorry had a long moustache with twirls at the ends. What a ridiculous looking moustache, he thought. As the vehicle approached, the moustache appeared to grow larger and larger until all he could see was the moustache speeding towards him.

He glanced to see Tom getting back to his position on top of an outcrop where he stood with his hands on his hips and an unpinned grenade hidden in the flap of his tunic. The first lorry rounded the bend and continued towards Tom's position but slowed to a crawl as the soldiers peered at him in confusion until the vehicle came to a stop below him. Without hesitation, he hurled the grenade, which exploded, and the men of Section 1 opened fire.

Waiting all day, Ned had felt as if time had slowed to a crawl, but now it moved too quickly. His ears were shocked by the almost simultaneous crack, crack, crack-k-k-k of rifle fire, sounding like a dry stone wall being pushed over. The tedium ended in a flash, breaking the trance that had settled on both the Auxiliaries and the Volunteers. He calmly steadied the butt of his rifle in the pit of his shoulder and placed his finger over the trigger.

When the grenade exploded, the vehicle veered off the side of the road as the driver lurched forward, blood pouring from his face.

Soldiers leapt out and ran to the south but were cut down by the men positioned there.

Wheel turn by wheel turn, the dust of the road kicking up into the gloom, the second lorry rounded the bend and stopped directly in front of Section 2 and Ned.

Ned felt his finger pulling the trigger as he heard a volley of shots ring out from Michael and the men on the other side of the road.

The soldiers shrieked, 'Fuck me, bastards. Get 'em!' A few of them jumped from the lorry and threw themselves on the ground and fired back at the men on the north side of the road, but they didn't see Ned to the south.

The driver of the lorry reversed about 25 yards and two men jumped out and made a dash back up the road. Ned followed them, watching their tunics flapping as they ran. One of them ran into the fallow field next to the house on the road. It was muddy and overgrown. Ned jumped from clump to clump keeping his eye on the man as he bobbed up and down in front of him. He found a dry rock from where he could see the whole field and watched as the soldier laboured through the mud.

Ned lifted up his rifle and took aim and fired but the man kept running. He pushed up on the cock, pulled back, pushed forward and down to load another round. Pulled the rifle back into his shoulder, looked through the sights, aimed at the back of his target and pulled the trigger. The soldier fell, his arms thrashing in the air as he came down with a thud.

He turned around to see where the second soldier had gone, as cracks of gunfire continued. The driver of the second vehicle was now dead, sprawled across the front seat of the lorry, but a soldier was underneath, firing at Section 2. He fell to one knee and took careful aim and fired one shot, two shots, three shots but the Auxie kept firing. Then again up on the cock, back, forward, aim, fire. This time his bullet found its mark and the soldier's body jumped as if pushed from underneath, his contorted torso crashed into the underside of the lorry and fell motionless on the unsealed road.

Several other soldiers were sprawled on the road firing their weapons, but one by one they were struck by bullets fired by Michael's Section. Having finished off the soldiers in the first lorry, Tom's Section were now moving quickly up the road, firing all the while.

As Tom reached the first dead soldier from the second lorry he shouted, 'Cease fire, cease fire,' and silence fell like a curtain crashing down. Then came the sounds of running feet and rustling belts and tunics. Ammunition stuffed in pockets rattled as the men from both Sections ran out to check that the Auxiliaries were indeed neutralised, motionless, slain.

Ned stood up and went over to the lorry where the man he had shot lay bleeding. He poked him with his rifle muzzle, his finger on the trigger, just in case. He was dead all right. He turned and ran back to where Tom and the others were also checking that the other Auxies were all dead.

'Where's Michael?' Ned asked.

'Didn't you see?' answered one of the men. 'Michael is dead, so is Jim O'Sullivan. Pat Deasy is wounded badly as well.'

Michael dead? How can I have missed it? Confused, he ran to where he had last seen Michael, crouched behind the rock, rifle aimed at the Auxies. There, two of his comrades stood looking down at the dead body of Michael. Ned stood beside them, and he too looked down on his dead friend. Michael's face was ghost white, his lips pallid. A red stain was in the middle of his chest, blood oozing out. His eyes were open and his mouth contorted, teeth gripped together askew, not straight. He hardly recognised the tortured face.

One man whispered, 'He's dead, man. Sure he's gone.'

Ned crouched down and touched his hands. They seemed so small, smooth but already waxy like a model made of clay, as if they had never been alive.

The two men grabbed Ned by the shoulders, pulled him up, but his legs draped beneath him like a rag doll. 'Come on Ned, stand up straight. We have to go now.' The three of them stumbled down over the rocks to the road strewn with dead bodies.

Men dashed back and forth collecting rifles, pistols and ammunition belts from the dead soldiers while others rummaged through the contents of the tenders. The sidecar soon came back up the lane and the collected weapons were placed inside it.

Tom stood in the middle of the road, a pistol in his hand and a rifle slung across his back. His green Volunteers tunic stood out in the near darkness as the only ray of colour visible in the dread scene, apart from splashes of sickening red.

His eyes darted from left to right and his torso swung from East to West as he observed the men collecting the Auxies' equipment.

Two men rushed up from the farmhouse where they had torn a door from its hinges to use as a stretcher for young Pat Desey. He lay on the road while one man knelt on his bandaged wound in an effort to stem the bleeding.

Ned looked around as the scouts that had been positioned on the road ahead, returned and took in the scene of carnage.

'All right men, fall in,' Tom bellowed and the men formed ranks one by one. 'Men, fall in,' repeated Tom in a deliberately deepened voice. Soon all movement came to a halt and the men left alive were formed into two lines standing at attention.

'By the left, quick march', called Tom. He paraded the men up and down and up and down. A few of the men were weeping, others looked determined. Ned felt... nothing. Was he even moving?

Left right, left right... attention... present arms... stand at ease.

'Men, enemy reinforcements may well be just a few moments away, so there is no time for slacking now. We have defeated the enemy here. Now our task is to make a safe withdrawal. DO YOU UNDERSTAND?'

'YES SIR,' the troop shouted in response.

'Fall out, and we'll make our way south.'

He sent two men to set the Crossley Tenders ablaze.

As the men clambered back over the rocks to where they had come from, into the darkness of the night, a harsh rain bit into their faces. The two blazing lorries lit up the sky in a deathly orange fire. The stench of burning oil and rubber filled the air like a poisonous elixir.

Ned remembered the uisce beatha he had shared with Michael in 1916 as they hid away in the hills by Gouganne Barra. He had felt the smokey creature then, sliding up his veins and releasing his innermost desires, the smoke that allowed him to dream, dream of love.

But the smoke that filled his lungs now was deathly, full of hate and despair. His friend was gone and Ned had committed murder, shot two men dead. He had abandoned all the good things in life and fallen for the trick of the devil. Tricked he was, for now he was as far from God as he could ever be.

Stumbling, falling, shivering but covered with sweat despite the biting cold, he walked on only because each time he hesitated the man behind crashed into him, as desperate as he was to get away from the scene of horror, the abandonment of God's will.

'Keep going, Ned. Don't stop.'

Pushed in the back, he stumbled forward unable to see, not because of the darkness or freezing rain, but because he felt alone, adrift, lost.

After several hours, they stopped for a five minute rest. They lit cigarettes and as the matches flashed glimmers of light onto his comrades, he saw the same thing in their faces as he now felt himself – fear, loathing, self-hatred. He had abandoned his friend. Michael lay cold, gone forever and now he was a killer. Cain he was.

Then Tom was beside him and looked in his eyes. 'Ned, I've seen this all before, in Mesopotamia. You've got to lose your desire. Just do what has to be done, and that is what you did. You did what you had to do. There's nothing more for it.'

Tom called the men towards him. 'We are near Manch Bridge, which is held by the Tans. So we have to cross the river with great caution.

'You are tired, hungry, wet and frozen. But you must put the ordeal we experienced today behind you. We defeated the enemy. We are nearly there, and we'll soon be met by the Ballincarriga Company. We just have to cross the Bandon River.

They waded through water tinkling over the pebbly shallows to the east of the low stone bridge. The lights of the Tan's vehicles illuminated the bridge, diffused through soft misty rain. Soldiers with rifles slung across their shoulders moved to and fro, looking into the water now and then. The smell of their cigarettes wafted down to the river beneath as the column crossed in silence.

They continued moving on and at midnight reached a farm at Granure near Ballynacarriga. Armed men greeted them. 'Well done, lads, well done,' they said, patting them on their backs as they ushered them into an empty barn strewn with straw. Their muddy boots scraped across the floor until they found a space and collapsed. Buckets of tea were ladled out and buttered bread given to all of them. Soon Ned was sound asleep.

He saw his mother, stirring the cauldron, steam billowing and red flames curling up from beneath the giant pot. Her shoulders moved back and forth, back and forth as she stirred. She turned around to look at him. 'Have you forgiven them?' she asked.

'Forgiven who?'

'Your enemies, of course.'

'How can I forgive them, after all they've done?'

'You have to forgive them, you must forgive them.'

'Why?'

'Because Jesus told us, told you, that you have to forgive your enemies or you will not be forgiven yourself.'

'Do you think they will ever forgive us, I mean now, after today? We beat them, defeated them. I know from playing football, we all forgive the boys who kick us in the shins as long as we win the game. But the ones who lose, they never forgive the ones that beat them.'

Ah well, sure wasn't that Ireland's problem for so long? We never won, and perhaps we were never able to truly forgive. But you blame yourself for Michael's death don't you? You're the one you need to forgive, aren't you?'

'I can never be forgiven now. I'm beyond redemption.'

'No one is beyond redemption, at least, not as far as we know. It's not for us to know who is redeemed or who isn't. God is the judge and Jesus told us we will all be redeemed if we believe in him. So you must forgive your enemies. Remember, you're a Christian first, a man second and Irish forever.'

****

Seán De Siun spent his early years in Australia before moving to London in the early 1970s.

His written works include non fiction redactions, documentaries, screenplays and short stories.

Also by the author and available from Fileata Fiction

Kings Road
The Curator
Caanice and the Book
Katie
Chatter

Copy Sales
Desire is available on **www.amazon.com**
Purchase direct from **www.fileata.co**

Made in the USA
Middletown, DE
20 March 2019